10 Things To Do Before I Go

CHANTELLE MATHEWSON

A 10 THINGS NOVEL BY CHANTELLE MATHEWSON

Trigger Warning:

This book contains sensitive material, such as:

Mental illness
Suicide
Explicit Sex
Foul Language
Reference to drug use

For all those readers out there searching for a reason to believe you are enough, you have found it. You were enough then. You are enough now. You always will be.

Chapter One

The waves breaking against the beach snatch my attention from the hoards of people rushing in off the last tour bus of the evening. From Aunt Milly's front porch I can make out each face. The adults are mostly cranky, their brows scrunched together and lips pulled tight. Most likely a result of too much time with their kids, who for the most part, are all still smiles and sunshine.

I am thankful for the ocean's interruption. I prefer to be looking at the vast blue expanse anyway, just a road and short beach away from Aunt Milly's front porch. I rock back on her creaky old porch swing and close my eyes for a moment.

Coming to Bar Harbor for the summer had been the last thing I wanted to do after dropping out of college and finding myself back home at my parents. I was completely comfortable making my old bed back up and sleeping everyday in the mild summers of Vermont. Mom and dad however, had other ideas. They'd been talking for years about renting out my room, and when I pulled my rusty Chevy into the driveway, I found that is exactly what had happened. A lanky college student by the name of Bill was wandering around my childhood room in a towel.

Aunt Milly's offer was suddenly extremely appealing.

"Stella," Aunt Milly's voice comes from behind me, musical and full of light. I look over my shoulder and for the tenth time since I got here this morning, I wonder how her and my mother are sisters. Aunt Milly is eccentric to say the least. She's tall, with bright blue eyes and long flowing blonde hair. I look like her in that way, except for the height. I take after my mom there, barely brushing five two. I also take after my mom's curves, being a bit too plump to be skinny but too thin to be plus sized.

Mom calls us perfectly mid sized.

"Dinner is ready, honey." Aunt Milly says, but instead of dipping back into the house, she sits down next to me on the swing and tilts her head back. "I am so glad you are here. It gets lonely in this big house."

I wish I could say the same. I wish I could say I am happy to be here, but I'm not exactly sure what I'm feeling. Surely, I never thought at twenty two years old that I would be a college dropout living with her strange Aunt in a picture perfect coastal town with no idea what I was doing with my life.

"It's beautiful," I settle on saying instead.

A loud crash and booming laughter yanks my attention across the road to where the tour bus just pulled away. A group of men my age are standing over a pile of bikes that have just fallen from their rack, and they are laughing with their heads thrown back.

There is nothing overwhelmingly unique about the group and I have almost looked away when I spot him.

He's standing a few feet away from the rest, his arms crossed over his chest. A giant smile fills his face, but from here, I'm not sure if it quite reaches his eyes. He's tall, but not lanky. He's got a swimmer's body. Even through his black t-shirt he is clearly muscled. His arms and calves are covered in tattoos (probably more of him too). I think it's the shoulder length brown hair that first caught my attention. Or maybe his indifference to the joke the others think is so hilarious. Either way, I can't stop staring.

"Don't even think about it." My Aunt's tone has hardened.

I glance up at her to see she's staring in the same direction I am. I raise an eyebrow, unsure what her warning means.

"Those boys are trouble," She tells me, shaking her head so her hair whips me in the shoulder. She clicks her tongue as we both watch them begin to gather the bikes back up as a group and place them back where they belong.

The one in the back begins tightening the cords, locking them all in place so they won't fall over again. He's chuckling and talking as he does to a redhead wearing a black ball cap who's knelt down beside him.

"Don't worry," I laugh, standing and stretching my stiff arms up into the air. I've been people watching for hours. My body screams to be moved. "I didn't come here to meet boys."

Aunt Milly stands with me and laughs as she leads me back inside.

"Of course you didn't. Not my Stella."

Her tone is endearing, but I find myself recoiling at it as I take one last look at the boy with the long hair and interesting tattoos.

I've never done the unexpected thing, until this spring. Not once did I skip school or bring a boy home. I'd only ever had one boyfriend - a relationship that ended on the worst of terms and convinced me to never try again. Compared to my siblings, I was a saint. Dropping out of college had come as such a shock to my parents, they thought I was joking at first. When they realized I wasn't, Aunt Milly's house for a reset was the best anyone could come up with.

I was not the girl who went to Maine for the summer and fell in love.

Good thing too, because there appeared to be enough good looking guys around here. Good thing I wasn't the kind of girl who cared.

Following Aunt Milly into her house, I close the screen door behind me.

"I probably made too much," Aunt Milly laughs, waving around her kitchen as if it's a buffet. It might as well be..

Each burner on the stove houses a pot, the counter full of different breads and desserts. It smells amazing and my stomach grumbles at the thought of eating any of it. She had said she was cooking something special, but I hadn't realized that meant she was also cooking for an army when there were only two of us.

"Are we expecting guests?" I ask with a chuckle, grabbing a paper plate from the stack and beginning to spoon homemade mac and cheese onto my plate. The cheese has that perfect pull. My stomach grumbles again.

"I'm just happy to have my Stell-Bell with me," winding an arm around my shoulder, she affectionately gives me a tight hug. I savor the contact for just a moment before she pulls away.

Aunt Milly had lived in Vermont for most of my childhood, right next door. It was only when Grammy passed away that she moved here to the vacation home Gram and had loved so much. When she did, it was almost as if a part of me was ripped away with her. I remember crying in my bedroom every night for a solid week. I even packed my bags, at fifteen years old, as I scrolled through my dad's work computer late at night looking for bus tickets.

It's nice to have her around again.

Aunt Milly and I are both quiet people. We make it through our feast with little talk and no awkward tension. She hums a quiet tune while we wash the dishes, and then I pad back out onto the front porch without a word.

I like not having to talk.

I was ten when I was diagnosed with social anxiety and fifteen when the doctor brought my mom into the room to announce my second diagnosis; depression. Aunt Milly, though only over phone calls and the twice a year visit, was the only one who really understood what a mental illness was.

Even I wasn't sure what was wrong with my brain until I was out of High School and learned no one is as put together as they seem.

The man with the long hair and tattoos is back, but he's alone this time. He's on the beach now, which in the dwindling daylight hours is beginning to empty. I watch as he drops a towel into the sand and settles down, pulling a bent and beaten book from the pocket of his cargo shorts and opening it up.

I wonder what he's reading.

The ocean breaks against the sand and the wind rustles gently in my hair. I can hear Aunt Milly whistling in the living room. My phone is vibrating in my pocket, but I ignore it.

I watch the man reading on the beach. I imagine the words going through his head, the images conjuring behind his eyes. I close my own and relax back into the comfort of the old porch swing.

I am totally fucked up. Life is totally fucked up. I focus on thinking about the book instead of the never ending stream of anxiety ridden thoughts plundering into my head.

Instead of thinking about every poor life decision that led me to this moment, I focus on elegant fonts and well chosen words. It works for a while, giving me a brief reprieve before the imaginary world in my head breaks and I'm pulled back to reality with a splash of water as the ocean breaks against the beach again.

When I open my eyes again to go inside, the man isn't sitting on the beach anymore, but his towel is still there.

I trudge up through the house, up two flights of stairs to the attic where my belongings are strewn around a beautiful guest room. The entire attic is mine for the summer, a sprawling space with floor to ceiling windows and plants in hanging baskets. A queen size bed sits against one slanting wall, dressed in fluffy white linens and too many pillows.

My bags, tattered and stuffed to the brim, look out of place strewn from the staircase to the foot of the bed.

I'll deal with them in the morning.

After dressing in shorts and a tank top, I crawl into bed, only to find the comfort unwelcoming. I toss and turn for what feels like an eternity.

How can I be twenty two with no clue what I am doing? I thought I would have my life together by now, but instead, I am spiraling into a lifetime of bad decisions and equally bad outcomes, and I have no idea how to deal with it.

It feels like just yesterday I was on my High School stage giving a valedictorian speech - no Stella. I can't think about how that ended. To blame my entire life after that point on what happened that day would be ridiculous. Ridiculous but exactly what I was doing. Before then, I was the perfect girl with the perfect dreams who was going to do perfect things.

I throw the blankets off and angrily stomp from the perfect room, down the perfect staircase, and out the perfect front door.

Everything here is perfect and I can't take it.

The waves of the ocean are high tonight. The moon casts a line down its tumultuous surface, leaving a wavering reflection in the blue.

I don't even realize I've stomped across the deserted road and onto the beach until I am sitting in the cool sand, my legs pulled up to my chest.

Many years of therapy have taught me how to sense a panic attack coming on. I can feel my chest tightening and my throat closing.

I suck in a deep breath and begin to gather five concrete things around me to focus on. The ocean, the sand under my fingers, a camp chair someone left propped against the fence, a light blue towel, and sitting on top of it, a tattered old book.

I glance around.

The beach is empty.

The man with the tattoos must be somewhere nearby. Maybe he dipped into one of the houses just off the beach, or maybe he's swimming, too far out in the dark water for me to see.

I crawl through the sand on my hands and knees and before I can stop myself, I'm opening the nameless book. It's made of leather, with swirled gold letters on the front reading Notes.

I flip it open.

The page I flip to is a list. It's the last page written on, with many before it, almost at the very end. The spine is bent in so many places, leaving the book always half open, dangling on any given page like a dare.

10 Things to do Before I Go.

I gulp as my eyes scan down the page.

Number One is underlined and bold, like the writer went over it with a pen until the ink bled onto the next page.

Learn how to smile without faking it.

I am stuck on that first bullet point, my eyes wanting to continue but my heart pleading with me not to. They slide disobediently down to the next line. This one isn't quite as bold and it's written in pencil instead of pen. It looks like it's been erased several times before the writer finally left it the way it is.

Finally finish that tattoo. Fuck, it's been 3 years.

I brush a finger over the page, feeling the indents where the pen and pencil dug in.

My eyes are about to move on when I hear footsteps in the sand nearby.

I slap the book shut and throw it onto the towel beside me, but it's too late.

Standing over me is a ruggedly handsome, extremely tall, tattoo covered man in black swim trunks, his hair pulled back at the nape of his neck.

He's dripping wet, his body gleaming in the moonlight. His head is cocked to the side and his eyebrows drawn together.

"Find anything interesting?"

Chapter Two

I think I am going to pass out.

Instead, I rise shakily to my feet and like the idiot I am, salute him. I actually salute him.

"Stella." I say, plastering a smile onto my lips.

"Oliver," He answers, bending down to pick up the book I was just nosily perusing through. He grabs the towel with it and wraps the book up in it before tucking it under his arm.

"I'm sorry," I stammer, running a hand through my hair. Stupid. I am so stupid. I have no excuse. What I just read was extremely personal, and I had no business looking at it. I gulp over my pride. "It's already forgotten. I barely even read anything."

He stares at me for a long moment.

His expression is unreadable. Is he angry or upset? Or neither? His lips are pulled into a tight line, but he's also biting down on one corner. His deep green eyes are unblinking as they stare into mine.

"You must be Milly's niece," He finally says.

I blink.

"Tourists aren't usually just sitting alone on the beach at midnight. Plus, you look just like her."

"I am. Her niece I mean," I play with my fingers, cracking my knuckles to refrain from biting my nails. "I'll go. Again, I'm sorry."

I turn to go but his wet hand grabs my arm.

I jolt backward and his hands fly up as if in surrender.

"I'm not mad," He finally says. He stands a good head taller than me, and he's towering over me now as he bends his head down to look into my eyes. "Tell me something about yourself."

"Excuse me?" My heart hammers in my chest.

"I think it's only fair," the corner of his mouth lips up in a smirk. "Come on. One thing."

I'm not sure if I should run or sit down. My fight or flight has unwillingly engaged, as it often does when I'm caught in a less than predictable situation. Quickly, I assess my surroundings. My perception isn't always reliable, but it feels as if my urge to run now is purely from how awkward I feel and has nothing to do with a real threat.

I just invaded this guy's space and he's standing here smiling, asking me about myself.

I should be hugging him. Not contemplating running away.

I gulp, looking anywhere but into his beautiful green eyes. They are making me nervous.

"Fine," I finally mutter. "It's a therapy technique. I was using your journal as one of five concrete things, and before I knew it I was opening it."

"Ah, the big five. Never worked for me." He sinks down onto the ground, the sand immediately clinging to his wet skin.

I want to brush it away.

"Get panic attacks often?" He sets the bundle of book and towel down next to him and stretches out on his back, closing his eyes.

Glancing around the dark beach, I'm not quite sure what to do. Town is dead. There are a few cars turning corners, a couple drunk couples laughing as they stumble up from a basement bar to their hotel. But for all intents and purposes, we are alone here.

I sink down next to him and pull my knees to my chest.

"I wasn't having a panic attack."

"Right. And my name's not Oliver."

I raise an eyebrow.

"I was in the water. Not dead."

Right. He saw the whole thing.

"It wasn't a panic attack. I was just… freaking out."

"It was impressive how quickly you pulled yourself together. Don't think I can do that."

"Yeah well, years of therapy," I laugh, my mouth popping open as soon as I realize what I've said.

But Oliver only laughs, opening his eyes to glance over at me.

"Don't worry," I sigh, shrugging. "It's not always that easy. If that makes you feel any better."

"Why would another person's suffering make me feel better?"

Again, my mouth pops open.

"I… I don't know," I stutter. "It's just something people say."

"It drives me nuts." His eyes slide shut again. "Someone else's pain will never bring me comfort. Well, I guess, some psychotic mass murderers would. Yeah, definitely, there's would."

My phone ringing in my shorts pocket startles me and causes Oliver's eyes to open again.

He's staring at me as I ignore the tone.

I know who it will be.

I have no interest in talking to them. Not right now. Possibly ever again.

"You gonna get that?"

I shake my head.

"Nope."

"Want me to get it?"

I laugh. Definitely not.

"No. Some things are just better left in the past."

"I don't think I agree with that." He says, sitting up this time and resting his arms on his knees. The waves crash, bringing the water further up the beach. "Everything always comes back somehow. You can't ever truly leave anything completely in the past."

Right. I'm not sure I'm in the mood for a mental breakdown right now, and the way this conversation is going, it is bound to happen.

I stand up and brush the sand off my legs.

He isn't looking at me anymore, but staring out over the ocean. I want to ask him what the heading in his journal meant. I want to ask him so many things, but instead, I swallow over the lump of questions in my throat and jut a thumb across the road.

"I'm exhausted."

"I'm sure I'll see you around, Stella."

He lays back down and closes his eyes. There is a moment where I just watch him. His chest rising and falling, his eyes twitching lightly as they move behind his lids. His stomach muscles flexing as he breathes. There is a moment where a small voice in the back of my head beckons for me to lay back down, feel the sand on my back, close my eyes and breathe with him.

Instead, I cross the road and head back to the perfect house, where I am the only thing fucked up.

*   *   *

I need to leave but my phone won't stop ringing. And I can't stop staring at it.

"Honey, just pick it up." Aunt Milly passes by the kitchen table, this time her arms loaded with empty boxes. She's making trips to her car so that we can leave for the diner she so graciously got me a job at for the summer. It's directly across from the small clothing boutique she owns, and the owner is a good friend.

"I can't."

"Want me to?"

I chuckle lightly, reminded of the same question coming from Oliver's mouth the night before.

"No."

"Who is it anyway?"

I glance up at her as she places the stack by the door and starts for the pantry again. She's got stacks of delivery boxes, some full and some empty, waiting in the back corner to go with her to the store. I was helping her before my phone began ringing and I sank down into one of her old wicker chairs, unable to move.

"Beth."

"Beth? As in Bethany Clay? Your best friend?"

"Former," I correct her.

"What? What happened? You girls have been inseparable since birth." With a worry line creasing between her eyebrows, Aunt Milly sinks down into the chair across from me, abandoning her task.

Inwardly, I groan. I don't want to talk about it. Because it's stupid. And when I say it out loud, I sound like a self obsessed idiot.

"Nothing happened," I shrug. "But Beth is going to med school. She's got a fiance and a dog and they are looking at buying a house. She doesn't want to talk to me."

Poking my phone, Aunt Milly chuckles.

"Honey, I think she does."

She thinks she does. She really wants to talk to High School Stella who was going to be a lawyer. She doesn't want to talk to present day Stella.

"It's not a big deal," I stand and shove my phone in the back pocket of my shorts. "Here, I'll help you with the rest of these."

I occupy myself with stacking the boxes still in the corner of the pantry. I can feel Aunt Milly's gaze on my back, but I try my best to ignore it.

She wouldn't understand, even if I tried to explain it to her. Mildred Brock has no idea what it's like to be less than at everything. I know she means well. So I do feel partially bad closing her off like this, but I can't just sit down and talk about my feelings right now. *Especially* not with her.

We load the car and drive in silence. In the passenger seat of Aunt Milly's brand new truck, I watch the scenery pass by.

The diner is a few miles down the road, still right on the coast. We drive slowly as tourists walk out in front of us without looking and locals slam on their horns.

Bar Harbor, Maine is beautiful. As caught up in my own selfish feelings as I am, I do realize that. I am lucky to be here, even if it is in less than ideal circumstances.

Cutting the engine in an off road parking spot labeled for employees only, Aunt Milly turns to look at me.

"Just try and be happy today, okay?" She reaches across the center console and tucks a strand of hair behind my ear. "If you do that, I think you'll really like it here."

Right.

Happy.

I smile and nod. Smile and nod.

"I've got these boxes. Don't want you to be late."

With a swift blow of a kiss, Aunt Milly hops out of the truck and distracts herself with the backseat. Taking that as my cue to leave, I head up the drive and around the front, jogging across the busy street to the ocean side diner I'll be spending most of my days at.

It's cute. The white paint on the dark wood is peeling in a few spots. A giant plastic lobster hangs over the front door, mocking me with its wide open eyes as I pass underneath it, the smell of fish and salt water wafting into my nose.

The diner is already open and in full swing, so I am hit with a sudden burst of laughter and music as the door closes behind me.

Taking a deep breath, I approach the hostess stand. A girl around my age, maybe a tad older, with bright red hair and dark eyeliner looks up from her seating chart.

"What can I do for you girlie? Table for one?" She pops her gum.

I shake my head. Is it too late to leave? Maybe sharing my old room back home with a gangly guitar player wouldn't be so bad.

"I'm supposed to start work today." I say instead. I've made it this far. Might as well suck it up and keep going. If I've learned anything at therapy, it would be that. "Oh!" Her eyes grow wide and she straightens up. "You must be Stella! Come on back!"

What is it with everyone here already knowing who I am? I knew Aunt Milly was a likable person, but I wasn't aware she apparently knew everyone and talked about me often.

"I'm Nat," she says as she weaves us through the crowds to the kitchen. "Lead server and hostess. Any questions, come ask me. You are gorgeous, by the way."

"Thank... thank you." I stammer.

She flashes me a smile as the kitchen doors swing open and then close behind us.

The loud laughter and music from the dining room is all but drowned out, replaced instead with yelling line cooks and clanking of plates.

I'm thrown head first into the rush of the day.

I've worked as a waitress since I was in High School, so I feel comfortable as I'm handed a menu to study, and then as I take drink orders and fill them.

Tucking myself away into the safety of my brain, I let my body run on autopilot for the rest of the shift. I meet more coworkers than I can remember the names of, Nat's really the only one seared into my head as I spend the shift glued to her side.

"Are you coming down to the HideAway tonight?" Nat is reapplying her lipstick in the reflection of the microwave in the back as the cooks pack away and clean up for the night.

I take a sip from my diet coke.

"What's that?"

Nat is gorgeous. Her hair is curly and perfectly done up. She's skinny and tall. But it's the confidence that makes her intimidating. If I hadn't spent all day trying to learn the menu and floor plan, I probably would have spent it feeling inadequate in her shadow.

"It's a bar. We're all going down once we leave here. You should totally come."

My anxiety could never. I try to formulate a polite way to turn her down without making it sound like I just don't want to go.

"Thanks for the invite," I smile, draining the rest of my drink and throwing the plastic cup in the trash. I glance at the door. Aunt Milly is probably waiting for me outside. "I told my Aunt I'd watch movies with her and just chill tonight."

Liar. Terrible liar. Aunt Milly doesn't even like movies. She calls them Satan's portal to your brain.

"Maybe some other time, then." Nat flashes me a smile and then saunters off to chat up a short blonde girl who's washing down a prep table.

I gather my things from the office and clock out while checking my phone. My heart sinks as I walk out of the diner. On top of the ten missed calls from Beth, there is also a message from Aunt Milly.

I had to bring Martha to the hospital. I'm going to stay with her until we know everything is alright. Are you okay to walk home?

Martha is her pregnant coworker, who's got no support system and lives in the office of the boutique currently due to being kicked out of her parents house. It would make me a terrible person if I said no.

It's only a two mile walk anyway.

Tell Martha I'm thinking of her. Leaving the diner now. I'll let you know when I'm home.

I could call an Uber. Or turn back and take Nat up on her offer.

Instead of doing either, I continue down the sidewalk, tucking my phone into my back pocket to remain present and looking at my surroundings. It's about ten. It was a long shift for the first day, but the tips were good and I'm feeling good, working again. It's been a couple weeks since I quit the small pub near campus. I like to work. It keeps my mind distracted.

The street lamps light my path. There are still cars on the road and a few groups of people walking about. I'm not completely alone. I'm not sure if I might prefer complete solitude.

I don't hear feet approaching from behind until a voice is calling out to me.

"Hey! Stella?"

I know who it is before I turn. When I do, Oliver is walking towards me with the red head he'd been talking to the first time I saw him. The redhead up close is just as tall as Oliver, and he has a kind smile. His attire is more laid back than Oliver's. He's wearing what appear to be swimming trunks, a t-shirt and a black ball cap. Up close I can see that the cap is worn in and tattered. There used to be writing on the bill but it's so worn I can't make out what it once said. Oliver beside him looks so put together in gray cargo shorts and a dark green button down.

"Hey, Oliver." I slow down, allowing for them to catch up to me, and then fall into step beside him, surprising even myself. I'm not sure why I didn't pick up my pace and pretend to be listening to music.

"Stella, meet Caleb. Caleb, Stella." Oliver waves a hand between us as we walk.

I wave a tiny wave, but Caleb completely stops in his tracks and holds his hand out for me to shake.

"How are you liking Maine, Stella?" He asks, that kind smile stretching over his face.

I shake his hand and then we continue walking.

"It's nice. Perfect." I answer, sure I'm the only one who can hear the sarcasm lacing my tone.

"We're headed to the HideAway. Wanna join?" Oliver stops walking and juts a thumb in the direction of a small flight of stairs leading to a basement door. A group of giggling girls is walking out.

"Thanks, but I'm exhausted. I just had my first day of work. I just want to crash."

"Oh, cool. Where are you working?" Oliver asks.

"Oceanside Diner," I tell him.

"No way," Caleb chimes in. "I work there on the weekends. I'll see you tomorrow then?"

"Yeah," I tell him, my hands growing clammy from the conversation.

"We'll let you get home then, but I have something I wanted to give you," Oliver reaches into the cargo pocket of his shorts and grabs out a book shaped wrapped package. It's wrapped in a paper bag with a giant S written on the front.

Hesitantly, I take it, my eyebrows knitting together.

"What is it?"

"You'll see," Oliver winks and my stomach does a flop. I can't help the small smile that tugs up the corner of my mouth. "Are you walking home?"

I nod.

"Here, let me walk you."

I shake my head.

"That's okay. Thank you though."

"Are you sure?"

"Really, I'm fine." I assure him, and because he doesn't look convinced, I continue. "It's only another mile and a half or so."

He bites down on his lip. Caleb catches the eye of someone about to walk into the bar and splits from us, giving me a small wave as he ducks away and into the bar. Loud music flows out for a minute before being silenced again as the door slams shut.

"Fine. But at least give me your number."

"Why?"

"So you can tell me you've made it home."

Why do you care? Is what I want to ask. Because why does he care? He just met me. And why do I care that he cares? I'm not here to meet boys. Definitely not tall, muscular, tattoo-covered ones who hand me gifts and offer to walk me home.

"Fine."

Grinning a wide smile, Oliver reaches into another pocket and pulls out his phone. Swiping up and over a few times, he hands me the glowing device with "add a contact" already pulled up.

I jot in my name and number and hand it back, quickly feeling the buzz as he sends me a message. I force myself to refrain from looking at it.

"Let me know what you think. Of the gift," He nods towards the package in my hand. It is clearly a book. But of what?

"I will." I tell him.

"See you around, Stella," He smiles, and to my embarrassment, he salutes me. My brain immediately goes back to last night on the beach and my inane introduction. Either he is mocking me, or he thinks he's being funny. Unsure which, I salute him back, and then turn with my cheeks burning red and don't look back until I am turning up the steps to Aunt Milly's house.

She's still not home.

I use my spare key and lock the door behind me.

As I lumber up to the attic, I send Aunt Milly a text letting her know I'm home, and then thumb over to the text Oliver sent me as we stood on the sidewalk.

OPEN IT.

I laugh, sinking onto the unmade bed and pulling the package onto my lap.

My fingers rip through the paper bag wrapper to reveal a leather bound notebook. It's new. As I thumb through it, there is only writing on the first page.

Ten Things To Do Before You Go

My heart is beating fast in my chest.

Grabbing my phone, I pull up Oliver's brand new contact and take a picture of the gift sitting on my knees.

I'm home. And by the way, what?

I send the picture off with the text attached and almost immediately get a reply back.

Thank you for letting me know. And by the way, journaling is for winners, Stella. Be a winner with me.

Laughing out loud, I sit my phone down and rifle through my half put away things before I find a black ink pen in the bottom of a backpack.

I lay down on the blankets and poise my pen to write, but my head is empty. There is nothing. What do I want to do before I go? And what does go even mean? Like, die, go? Or like, move, go?

I almost text Oliver and ask.

I almost text Oliver and tell him I'm lonely.

I almost call Beth and tell her I'm lonely.

I almost do a lot of things. But instead, after twenty minutes of staring at the blank, mocking page, I close the book and sit it with its pen down on my bedside stand.

I plug in my phone and shrug into the blankets.

How am I supposed to know what I want to do before I go when I barely know what I want to do tomorrow? Right now, all I know is that I want to talk to Oliver again. And I'm not sure why, but the thought of it leaves a gaping hole in my chest.

I fear that somehow, life isn't going to ever quite be the same again.

Rolling over and closing my eyes, I push the thought away. It's just a journal and Oliver is just a man.

So why do I already feel so empty at the thought of not having either?

Chapter Three

Aunt Milly never came home last night. This morning, there was a voicemail left on my phone. They might have to do an emergency c-section on Martha's baby, so Aunt Milly is staying the night.

So I drove myself to work.

Because I am always so afraid of being late for everything, I arrived half an hour early. Which means I am now sitting in my car, staring at the first page of the blank journal Oliver gave me.

At least now there is a one written on the first line, right under the heading, circled in black ink.

My first thing to do before I go.

I bite down on my lip as I begin writing.

Wear more skirts. I write. *I like skirts.*

I doubt that's what he meant by things I want to do. I wish I could continue reading his list.

Pushing the last bite of my bagel into my mouth, I chew slowly as I stare at the page.

2. Stop being so afraid of talking to people.

I pause and cross it out.

Stop being so afraid of everything.

A sharp rap on my window jolts my head up and causes me to slam the book shut and shove it between my seats. Nat is standing there, waving excitedly.

She points to the passenger seat and before I can react, is jogging around the car and yanking the door open.

"You have got to try this." Taking a seat, she shoves her iced coffee into my hand. It's extremely light colored and looks very sweet.

I take it and put the straw to my lips as she watches me eagerly like a puppy dog. An assault of sugary flavors heavily overpowered by caramel attack my tongue.

"Amazing, right?"

I hand it back.

"Super sweet." I say.

She giggles, sweeping a strand of her curly hair out of her face.

"I love weekends. The tips are always mwah. Chefs kiss." She leans back and looks over at me. "You should really come to the bar with us tonight. I promise, it is so much fun."

"I don't know," I shrug and then add honestly. "Bars aren't really my thing."

Her mouth pops open.

"Come on. Bars are everyone's thing."

I laugh, because who is she hanging out with who loves bars that much? I wonder if she knows Oliver. I clear my throat and tuck a strand of wayward frizz behind my ear.

"Will Oliver be there?"

She wiggles her eyebrows at me. So she does know him. And apparently now thinks I have a thing for him. Shit. I should have kept my mouth shut. Why did I even open it? I'm so stupid.

"He's always there on Saturdays. So hot, right? Don't worry," She shoves her left hand in my face where a shiny, large rock is gleaming. "I'm engaged. The wedding is in a month. When she gets back from overseas. She's in the army. But she'll be home for a week. It's gonna be super cute."

"Oh. Congratulations."

"Thanks! Hey, you should totally come." She takes a long sip from her coffee. "Her name's Carrie. She's a total badass. You would love her."

"Okay."

How does Nat know if I would love her? She barely even knows me. And even more disturbing of a thought, why do I suddenly really want to go to this wedding and meet this girl?

I shake out my shoulders.

While totally on board with the decision, Mom warned me about coming here. "Maine does weird things to you, Stella. The people there are just different. If you don't watch out, you might just fall in love and never come back."

That was not what was happening here.

"Can I have another sip?" I ask, purely to yank myself from my thoughts.

With a wide grin, Nat shoves the coffee back in my hands and I ignore the assault of sugar as I take a long pull from the cold cup.

We head into work shortly after, Nat leading me with her bubbly step and loud Hi to every passerby. Grabbing my hand, she tows us through the already overwhelming crowd.

Our shift began earlier today and ends earlier. We won't be working dinner rush, but we do have breakfast and lunch.

As I tie on my apron and study the menu, a familiar red head pops up beside me and leans on the prep table I'm in front of.

"Hey! We're in the same section." He nods towards the white board chart on the wall. I'm on my own today, which makes me happy. I prefer to work on my own. Even if it is only my second day.

"I might need a little help," I laugh, tucking my pens and order book into the pocket of my apron and tightening the band on my pony tail.

He stands and places a hand over his heart.

"Stella, I solemnly swear to help you make it through this shift. Come hell or high water."

Funny. Caleb is funny.

"Just don't let me drown."

"Never," he laughs, and then moves on to the drink station to fill himself a cup of sprite.

The shift starts quickly and never slows down.

Nat spends a lot of time behind the hostess stand on her phone, while Caleb spends a lot of time flirting with every waitress and cook he can. Everyone seems to like it. He's got a very loud and bubbly personality. He and Nat are very alike in that way. It's fun, but for a person like me, it's also very draining.

When the shift comes to an end, I'm counting out my tips by the time clock as the dinner shift comes in to set their things down and clock in.

Caleb and Nat walk back together, laughing and bumping into each other.

"Come on, Stella. We're not giving you a choice tonight. You are coming with me." Nat grabs my hand.

"Way to force the girl," Caleb is stuffing his feet into sandals and shoving his work shoes under the desk. Grabbing that tattered old hat he always wears from the coat rack, he turns to smirk at me. "Just come for a bit. If you don't like it, you can totally leave."

Nat leans close to my ear so her breath is tickling my lobe as she giggles and only I can hear her.

"I texted Oliver. He is totally gonna be there."

I swallow hard over the lump in my throat, unsure if that info makes me want to go more or less. I want to talk to him, but I don't want to talk to him. It makes no sense and it's hurting my brain. I'd rather just go home and crawl into bed.

"Fine," I finally grumble. "I'll go. But just for a bit. I am exhausted."

"Victory!" Nat thrusts a fist in the air as Caleb laughs and shakes his head at her.

We join the hoards on the sidewalk and instead of heading for our cars, continue down the pavement towards the bar. We smell like diner but at least there isn't a strict dress code. Although if I had to pick what I'd wear to a bar, it wouldn't be my old faded denim shorts and a high necked black t-shirt. I pull my hair down as we walk and comb my fingers through it.

"You look great," Nat laughs, pulling her fingers through my hair on the other side. How does she still look like a goddess? I'm pretty sure she must sweat glitter.

The steps down to the bar are steep and well worn. Caleb holds the door open for us and we disappear into the dark interior of the building, met with dancing bodies and loud music. It isn't too crowded in here yet, but it's barely five at this point. I don't really have any interest in seeing what it's like in here past nine.

I notice Oliver before he notices me. He's sitting on a stool at the bar with a glass of water in his hand. He's talking to the bartender and is completely surprised when Caleb slaps him on the back and takes the stool next to him.

"Hey!" Oliver greets the group of us over the too loud music before his eyes land on me. Is it just my imagination, or does his smile widen a bit? "Stella. Did you like my gift?"

Nat, obviously already bored with the conversation, rolls her eyes and takes out her phone. I see Carrie's chat bubble pop up and then Nat is weaving through the crowd with her phone to her ear.

I focus back on Oliver.

My ears are ringing. A blazing pain has started behind my eyelids. It's too loud in here. I am not the girl who just randomly goes to a bar. And for what? To see Oliver? That is the only reason I am here.

I can feel the panic rising in my chest in the form of quick, short breaths and a rapid heartbeat. I press my palms together and pinch at the space between my thumb and pointer finger on my right hand, focusing on the feeling as I stare into Oliver's beautiful green eyes. He's waiting for me to answer.

"I'm sorry. What?"

"The gift. Did you like it?"

I want to answer him, but it's so loud in here and I can't focus. I can barely even breathe. Caleb is flirting with the busty bartender, Nat is in the back corner waving her free hand around as she talks, and everyone else is talking too loudly. Who did I think I was, coming here?

"Sorry. I gotta go."

I turn on my heel and weave my way through the moving bodies, keeping my eyes glued to the door. When I finally reach it, I burst out into the warm evening air and up the steps. I don't stop until I reach a bench on the street and collapse into it, my head falling into my hands. People are walking by - the world is moving around me. Noises and smells and laughter.

I focus on my breath. In and out.

A large hand rests on my back and rubs slow circles across it. I glance over. How long has Oliver been sitting there? Did he follow me out?

"Sorry…" I manage, prying my head up from my hands. He shakes his own head, his eyes concerned.

"Please stop apologizing." He pauses for a moment, his hand the only thing I can feel. I focus on it and my breathing while still ragged, becomes a bit easier to command. "Do you want to go for a drive with me?"

My Aunt's words go through my head.

She warned me about him. She warned that he was no good, bad news she had said.

But right now, at this moment, all I know is that I need to get out of here. I need to be where it is quiet and for some reason, I want that place to be with Oliver.

"Yeah," I finally say. "Let's go."

He stands first and offers me his hand to hold. I take it, welcoming the warmth as it engulfs my smaller one. He leads me through the bodies on the sidewalk, keeping me pinned closely behind his back.

I don't realize he's taking us to his truck, parked alongside the road a few buildings down, until he is reaching into his pocket for his keys.

"My car is just down the road." I say.

"We can take your car," he turns to look at me, mid retrieval of his keys. "I want to take you to this lookout a few miles out of town. It's up a ways, that's all."

"Oh," I swallow. "Okay. Your truck is fine."

"Do you want to drive?"

I shake my head.

"That's okay."

His eyes search mine for a moment. My breathing is still coming short and staggered. What is he looking for? Is he finding it? He stares a bit longer and when he talks again, his eyes have softened a bit.

"You can trust me, Stella." He says.

I search his eyes for what I fear is longer than normal. He's standing with one hand in his pocket, the other still holding mine. There are people moving around us, cars driving, my chest rising and falling a bit too fast. I can not find a single reason not to trust him. Except the ever looming thought of Aunt Milly's words nudging at the back of my head. I push them away.

"You barely know me," I blurt out. "Why do you want to hang out with me?"

Shit. Fuck. Shut up, Stella. I want to actually kick myself in the face.

He seems completely unphased, his expression barely changing. The only change is a slight rise of the corner of his mouth and tilt of his head.

"You invaded my privacy and haven't left my head since. I tend to take shit like that as a sign."

Fuck.

My heart skips a beat and it has nothing to do with the panic attack edging to the back of my vision.

"Oh." The noise is more like a gust of air out of my mouth than an actual word.

"Come on." He tugs my hand and opens the passenger door, waiting for me to climb into the cab.

His truck is nice. It's a mess inside and smells like a mix of pine and coffee. I settle into the comfort of the familiar smells and wait for Oliver to walk around the front and climb in next to me.

"Where are we going?" I ask.

"You'll see." He flashes me a smile. "I promise, you'll like it."

Chapter Four

The drive is quiet. His radio isn't playing and neither of us reaches to fix it. I wonder if he always drives in silence. I hope he does.

Oliver took his hand back from mine to get into the truck, and I feel empty without it. His rests near the center console. It would be so easy to grab. If I were a girl like Nat, or Beth, I would do just that. I would make a move. But I'm not. I am Stella. And Stella doesn't make the first move. She swallows her tongue and watches out the window at the scenery as a drop dead gorgeous man who apparently can't stop thinking about her sits not an arm length away.

He turns the truck off the road about two miles outside of the bustling tourist town. We bump onto a back road lined with trees and continue, driving slower now.

I texted Aunt Milly when we left Bar Harbor and told her I was going out of town with someone from work. It was only half a lie. She told me to have fun and let her know when I was headed home. She doesn't need to know that I'm with the only person she's warned me against.

Oliver slows the truck to a stop and puts it in park. We are in the middle of the woods and there is nothing around. I raise an eyebrow.

"Is this where you take me to die?" I am only half kidding.

He laughs and rolls his eyes, illuminated lightly by the glow of the moon through the trees.

"Come on."

I follow him against the nagging voice in my head telling me not to.

There is a well trodden path cutting through the trees that was all but invisible from the truck. Plus, once I am outside, I notice we are in fact parked in what looks like a well used turn off. There is even a sign pointing to the trail he is taking me on.

So maybe not a murderer.

The trail is winding and short.

When it ends and he steps to the side so I can walk around him, my jaw pops open.

We are standing on the edge of a cliff that drops directly into the ocean. There is a flimsy wooden fence standing between us and the lapping waves. We are high up, but they are rough tonight, reaching halfway up the cliffside. The moon glows above the water, hidden partially by clouds. It's only a little after seven now, so the sun isn't completely fallen below the horizon yet, leaving a dull pink dusting over the water.

"It's beautiful." I sink down onto the dirt and pull my legs up against my chest.

Oliver sinks down next to me.

"I like to come up here to clear my head. During the day it's bombarded by tourists. At night, it's like people forget about it."

"Not you," I glance over at him and he's looking at me. "I started writing in the journal you gave me. What does that mean?"

"A journal?"

"The heading. Ten things to do before you go?"

He smiles and runs a hand along the edge of his jaw. There is a 5 o'clock shadow growing there. His hair is down, grazing his shoulders. I notice a rose covering the expanse of his left hand as he brushes it over his face and resist the urge to reach over and touch it. The artist did such a good job. Although black and white like all of his tattoos I've seen, it looks so real.

He digs into his cargo shorts and out comes the journal, bent and hammered.

"I started writing these lists in High School," he says. "When I was sixteen. The format of the list is like a tribute to the first journal I ever wrote. I've written many lists since then, but I always start it the same way."

"Why?"

I know I'm asking a lot of personal questions and he has no reason to answer them. Yet he does. And he doesn't seem to mind. He isn't looking at me, but down at the book in his hands. The way he holds it makes my heart ache for him as much as it makes me want to take it and continue reading it. Part of me thinks he would let me.

"I don't feel the same way sixteen year old me did. I don't want to be gone as much as he did. But it's always possible to slide back there. And I never want to forget him, you know? He went through a lot to get us here."

I gulp.

"So by before I go, you mean like, suicide?"

He nods.

"I did, then. It means something different to me now."

"And when you wrote it in mine?"

"Well," he places his journal down in the dirt between us and looks over at me. "What does it mean to you?"

"I don't know."

He is so close to me. It would be so easy to close the distance between us. Hold his hand. Kiss his lips.

"Want to know a secret?" I ask him instead, the words coming out in a whisper.

He nods.

"I will never turn down a secret."

"You can't tell anyone."

He makes a locking motion over his lips and throws the imaginary key into the ocean. It's corny, but my heart skips another beat.

"I would never betray your trust, Stella."

He keeps saying all of the right things, and my brain and heart can't take it. I feel giddy. I'm not sure if I love it or hate it.

I ignore the giddy feeling his words gave me and focus on what I was going to say instead. He's baring his soul to me, so it is only fair I at least half do the same.

"I never feel like I am enough," I mutter, looking down into the dirt and tracing a star just above the journal. I trace and retrace as I speak, making the lines deeper and deeper. "That's why I came here. I dropped out of college and quit my job. I was supposed to be the daughter who did everything right. You know? Instead, I'm just a disappointment. But, I get here and… everyone here is so perfect. Which is definitely not helping. I'm not sure what to do anymore."

Silence follows for several long moments before Oliver's hand grabs mine and stops the tracing. He holds it lightly in the dirt and I don't pull away. I like the way it feels, and I appreciate that I didn't have to make the first move.

"Can I make a suggestion?"

I nod.

"Be my friend."

I laugh but he continues, looking over at me with a gleam in his eye and slight smirk on his lips.

"I am serious. Just give friendship with me and the people I hang out with a good try. You'll notice quickly that this place isn't nearly as perfect as it seems."

"And that will make me feel better?"

"No," He tilts his head to the side. "Probably not. But it might make you feel a tad bit less alone."

"Why are you even trying to help me? Shouldn't you be like, mad at me?"

"Why would I be mad at you?"

"In your words, I invaded your privacy."

He laughs and squeezes my hand. It sends a tingle directly to my stomach which radiates outward and fills my entire body. I squirm, unsure why his touch makes me feel so many things and unsure how to make it stop.

Or if I even want to.

"I can be mad at you, if you'd like. I find it easier to just move on though. If I was going to be mad at someone for reading it, I shouldn't have left it on the beach."

I suck in a long and deep breath, blowing it out through my nose as the silence settles back around us.

"Fine." I finally say into the growing darkness. "I will give being your friend a shot."

"Good," he nudges his elbow gently into my ribs, his hand still holding mine firmly. "Anyway, my intentions might not be completely selfless."

"What do you mean?"

"I'll take any excuse to keep seeing you."

Heat floods my cheeks and I am sure I am bright red. Thank God it is getting dark out. I look down and bite on the corner of my lip.

When I look back up, Oliver is looking at me in a way that makes me want to curl up into myself and never come out. He is looking at me like I am something special.

I want to convince him I'm not. I want to tell him to take a step back before he realizes I am terribly broken and there is no point in trying to fix me. I want to do every single thing I can think of to push him away.

Instead, I squeeze his hand and stand up, dragging him up with me.

"Does this town have any more hidden gems?"

I'm not talking about the lookout, but he will assume I am as I nod towards the cliff.

"Loads."

"Good. I want to see them all."

*   *   *

I cut the engine in front of Aunt Milly's house, my breath quickening as I see her form sitting on the front porch. It's past ten. I'm not even sure where the night went. Oliver and I walked the trails around the lookout for what felt like a few minutes, returning to his truck two hours later. I don't even remember half of what we talked about.

"What is your favorite animal?" I asked him as we came to the end of the trail.

"Rhinos," he had said, glancing back at me with a sadness in his eyes I didn't recognize. "I did a paper on them in middle school and they've stuck with me ever since. Did you know they are going extinct?"

I shook my head and his eyes lit up with a new fire as he passionately began telling me every rhino fact he knew, ending in the fact that his favorite color has been gray ever since then.

"Gray is an underrated color," he shrugged. "Just like rhinos are an underrated animal. In my middle school brain, loving the color the animal is meant I was doing something for them."

I think that part of the conversation stuck with me even as I got out of my car because of the way his expression clouded with sadness. His empathy made me want to wrap my arms around him and never let go. Even as I replied with a weak - "my favorite animal is an owl. Because they're pretty."

He'd chuckled and we'd moved on.

I also remember the feel of his hand in mine as we walked, guiding me around roots and stumps that blocked the path in the darkness.

I snap my attention from my memories and to the path in front of me as the glow from the porch light illuminates a soft pool on the sidewalk.

Aunt Milly watches me as I walk up the front steps, her eyes following my path.

"Hey Honey," She says.

"Hey."

"Your mom called tonight. I told her you went out with some friends after work."

"Oh," I dig into my pocket. I do have two missed calls from her. "Is everything alright?"

"She just wanted to check in." She takes a sip from her mug. It's probably tea. "Who'd you meet at work?"

I bite down on my lower lip.

"Nat. And Caleb," I lean up against the porch railing, considering my options. "Oliver was there too."

Aunt Milly's expression doesn't change. It's unreadable, which is even worse.

"Nat is a nice girl." She finally says. "Be careful with those boys. I don't want to see you getting hurt."

"Is there something about them I should know?"

She pauses, and for a moment, I think she's about to tell me something important. Her brow pulls together and her lips part. Instead, she shakes her head.

"It's not my story to tell Stell-Bells."

"Okay," I nod. If she wants to be vague, I can be too. "I'm exhausted. I'm gonna call it a night."

"Goodnight, honey."

I blow her a kiss and then walk away, up to the attic where my still unpacked bags are waiting for me.

I change into sweats and pull the journal from my bag, settling down onto the middle of the bed.

3. I scribble. *Stop falling for Oliver. You idiot.*

My phone begins vibrating where I sat it next to me on the bed. I glance over.

Beth's face is beaming up at me. Her contact photo is an old one. I took it in High School and have made it her photo every time I got a new phone. Her jet black hair is pulled up into two braided pigtails, she's wearing way too much red lipstick, and she's smiling so wide her eyes are squinting. It was our freshman talent show and she sang to a country song she barely knew the words too. It was terrible, but it made her so happy.

As if moving on their own, my fingers reach over and grab the glowing device, pressing the green answer button and holding it to my ear.

Shocked silence follows before Beth's voice fills the room and I close my eyes.

"Hey, Stella," she says softly.

"Hey." I swallow over the huge ball currently lodged in my throat. "What's up? I'm kind of busy."

"Oh. I just… I'm glad you answered."

"Do you need something?"

Silence again. It's like a gut punch, forcing out the opposite of what I actually want to say. How do you tell your best friend since childhood that life didn't pan out like you thought it would? How do you tell her you aren't the girl she became best friends with? How do you tell her any of that without her turning her back on you?

The answer is you don't.

You turn your back first to save you both the pain.

"No. How have you been? It's been forever since we last talked. So much has happened."

Terrible. Struggling. Barely surviving.

"Good. I've been good. You?"

Her response is too quick and entirely fake. I know her better than I know myself, and her answer breaks my heart.

"Good. Really good."

I bite down on my lip, contemplating what I am going to say. The tears are welling up in the corner of my eye. I wipe one away as it dares to drop.

"We're both lying, aren't we?" I finally whisper.

Her only answer is a relieved sigh. Shit. I should not have opened my mouth.

"Stella-"

"I have to go."

I hang up and the sobs take over my body before the phone has even hit the bed. I grab the journal and scribble in messy writing.

4. Stop being such a shitty fucking friend.

And then I throw the journal across the room.

Chapter Five

"Where did you go last night?" Nat's hair is braided perfectly down her back. We have the same shift again today, only this time, it's just breakfast and brunch. I think it's quickly going to become my favorite shift. I get out right after noon, which means I am going to have the whole second half of my day to go down to the beach.

I haven't been able to since I got here and I am really looking forward to it.

Breakfast today is going slow. We aren't too busy, so as I wait for a new pot of coffee to brew, Nat is pestering me about last night.

She wiggles her eyebrows at me.

"I noticed Oliver was gone too."

"Nothing happened," I tell her, keeping my tone light. Caleb is here somewhere too, and I don't need him hearing me talk about his best friend. I don't need him going back to Oliver and telling him how obsessed I already am. I'm not obsessed. Nat brought it up.

"Nothing? Meaning you weren't with Oliver or meaning you were with Oliver and it stayed PG?"

"The second one," I mutter, pulling the coffee basket out as it finishes brewing and tossing the filter in the trash.

Nat's eyes widen and she nudges me in the arm.

"First week in town and you already have the eye of Oliver Brenton. Go you!"

I pause for a moment, looking around to make sure no one can hear us. Specifically a certain redhead who's spent the morning telling me my hair looks extra blonde today and complimenting me on my eye makeup. I've only known Caleb two days and it is becoming very obvious that he is a serial flirt.

When I confirm we are alone in the back besides the cooks noisily chatting in the kitchen, I look back at Nat and clear my throat, keeping my tone light.

"Is there anything about Oliver I should be worried about?"

"What do you mean?"

"My Aunt…" I trail off, almost losing the nerve to ask the question again. But Nat's eyes are wide and she is listening intently. It's hard not to trust someone like Nat. "She mentioned something about being careful. Twice, actually."

Nat looks away for a moment and in that second, I catch a look in her eye I don't recognize. It's not as happy and airy as she normally is. But it's only there for a moment, and then it's gone.

When she looks back, she straightens and grabs the pot of coffee I finished brewing, pouring some into her styrofoam coffee cup from this morning. Her lips are drawn tight together.

"I love Milly," She starts. When she puts the pot back, she does it a bit too roughly and coffee sloshes up and over the sides. "I do. But she hasn't lived here her whole life. She keeps to herself. And she doesn't know everything that goes on in this town."

I think she's done and am about to apologize for whatever I said that upset her when she continues.

"She should keep her opinions to herself is all I am saying. And if you want to know more about Oliver, ask him. It's none of my business."

"Sorry," I say quietly. "I didn't mean-"

"Don't be sorry," Nat's joking, light hearted tone is back. She takes a swig from the coffee that I know must be burning her mouth and wraps her other arm around my shoulder, pulling me close. "I just mean to say that Oliver is a great guy. He's just got some baggage. Don't we all?"

With that she saunters off to the dining room, leaving me alone by the coffee machine to ponder over what just happened.

I don't have long though before Caleb is stopping me in the middle of the dining room as I walk back from a table with an empty tray. He links his arm with mine and begins to skip, tugging me along with him.

I laugh against my will.

Caleb has that effect, I am beginning to realize.

"You coming to my place tonight?"

"Excuse me?"

Caleb laughs, stopping us once we've reached the kitchen again and spinning me around in front of the drink machine. I step to the side as he begins to fill a drink order. How does he possibly make waiting on tables look like fun? I'm not sure, but he does.

"I'm having a party. There's gonna be beer, pizza. I live right on the beach. Oh and I don't know if I mentioned it," he pauses, wiggling his eyebrows. "But Oliver is my house mate."

"Does everyone know he and I hung out last night?" I yell whisper, the sound coming out choked and high pitched.

He laughs, patting a hand on my shoulder.

"This town might be full of new people every day, Stella, but the ones who live here are in everyone's business. Plus, I live with the guy."

Was he talking about me?

I want to ask but my anxiety could never.

"Here, give me your phone." He says and before I've even gotten it fully out of my pocket, he's grabbed it and found my number in settings. Then he's on his own, texting me. He then adds his name into my phone all in a few seconds. I glance down at the message.

He's given me their address.

It's right across the street from mine. Which makes sense as to why Oliver was out on the beach so late at night when we first met. His house must be one on that side of the road, directly leading down to the sand.

"You should stop by. It'll be fun."

I work the rest of my shift trying my best to avoid both Nat and Caleb. I have done enough socializing for the morning, and while I like them both, I don't think my social battery can take much more right now.

I go to the bathroom at the end of my shift and make sure to stay in there until I no longer hear their loud laughter and voices in the kitchen.

Clocking out, I leave just as quickly, making a beeline for my car. I feel bad avoiding them like this. But I need time to recharge. Especially if I am even going to consider going to Caleb's tonight.

Am I? Considering it I mean. I'm not sure.

Aunt Milly is still at the boutique when I get home. It's only mid day and the sun is still high in the sky. It's a beautiful day. I've been lucky so far with perfect weather this summer. Because I know it's not likely to last, I am going to savor every moment of it.

I change into a bathing suit. It's my favorite, a simple black bikini that Beth helped me pick out two summers ago. I've put on a little bit of weight since then, so the straps cut in a bit on my hips and back, but I still like it. I look like my mom when I look in the mirror. Full and beautiful.

Looking through my clothes for something to put over it, the journal from where I threw it to the floor and haven't picked it back up mocks me.

Inside, there is a line I wrote. Wear more skirts.

My fingers dance over a pink skirt with little gray flowers that I bought last summer and still haven't worn. It's not that I don't like the way skirts look on me. I do. It's something else, something I don't really like to think about much. It's a silly problem, in the grand scheme of things. And when I think about it too much, I convince myself I'm an idiot for letting it bother me.

I haven't worn a skirt since senior year of High School when Leo Landerson, the first boy I ever kissed, made fun of the way my pencil skirt made my stomach look in front of the entire school. That morning, he had praised how beautiful my body was while touching every inch and then that afternoon called me a cow on stage during assembly while I stood at the microphone, mid speech, completely speechless.

I am a completely different girl than I was then. Yet, that doesn't mean I've kissed a boy since. That doesn't mean I've trusted a boy since.

"Who could ever actually be attracted to that?" Leo laughed, facing the entire student body with that charmingly devilish grin on his lips.

I can still remember how his hands felt on my body as he begged to fuck me. I can still remember the praises he sang as I gave him a blow job. I can still remember the way I almost gave him myself as he told me how beautiful I was. I can remember it and now, I feel like an idiot as my cheeks flame bright red and a choir of laughter echoes through the auditorium. Was he just mad that I may win valedictorian and not him? He had told me he was fine with it either way. Was that what this was about?

I stood like a statue as he continued to mock me, laughing at me, gesturing at my body as if I was a piece of discarded meat. I felt the tears running down my face but I couldn't stop them.

I suck in a deep breath, yanking myself from the memory before I get too deep.

It's a skirt. It is not a boy named Leo. It is just a skirt. And Leo is far away from here.

I won valedictorian anyway, which is a small constellation compared to the trauma he left me with, but one I've held on tightly to since.

I tug the skirt on, ripping off the tag as I do. Already too much in my thoughts for one day, I grab the first tank top my fingers find and yank that on too. Last minute, I grab the journal from the floor and wrap it in a towel before I head down across the road and to the beach.

It's pretty full with families and couples, laughing, running around and swimming.

I lay my own towel down in a pretty empty corner of the beach. I strip down to the bathing suit and settle down onto the towel, letting the warm sun sink into my skin as I bask in its light.

My phone dings just as I've gotten comfortable.

I groan and grab it from my pile of clothing.

My mom's name lights up the screen with just a simple, Call me, texted out.

I sit up and dial her number. My family has always been pretty close. My older brother, Daven, and my younger sister, Elsie, both still live in Vermont. Elsie is only seventeen and still lives with mom and dad. She's the perfect daughter. She's even taking college courses already through her High School. Daven is one year older than me at twenty three. He lives about half an hour from my parents with his pregnant wife, Malory. When my mom suggested that I come here for the summer, every single jaw dropped, because she was famous for wanting her babies all within walking distance.

I am still not entirely sure why she suggested it.

Sure, my room was taken. But Daven had plenty of space and had even offered his spare room to me. The only deciding factor on me coming here had been the temptation of seeing Aunt Milly again.

I was extremely close to my mom and dad growing up, not just my siblings. My mom was almost as much my best friend as Beth was.

But things changed once I went to college.

We stopped talking as much, and when I did go home for breaks, she was closed off, distant. Don't even get me started on the conversations I had with her about my mental health and school.

As much as I love my parents, it is a fact that neither of them believe in depression or anxiety. They think everything can be fixed with some hard work and elbow grease.

Maybe that's why they pushed me here.

They realized they couldn't fix me.

Now that my mom is trying to get a hold of me, the worst jumps to mind. I haven't even been here a week. What could I have possibly done wrong already?

She picks up on the second ring.

"Hey, Stella."

"Hi mom. What's up?"

"I was just checking in to see if you still planned on coming home for Malory's baby shower."

Shit.

"When is it again?"

"Next week, honey."

Fuck.

"I'll have to see if I can get it off work. I completely forgot."

"Work? Good for you honey. Where are you working?"

"Oceanside Diner."

"Oh." She can't hide the disappointment in her voice. "Well, is the pay good?"

"The tips are." I say, chewing on my nail and drawing blood. I stop, stuffing my hand under my leg to keep from gnawing on it any more.

"Good. Did you hear Elsie got into the summer program through the college? She'll be earning two credits. And she's got a job helping with clerical work at the Vet. You know the one on East Street?"

"That's awesome mom."

"It is. Tell your Aunt Milly I said hi."

"I will."

There is a long, awkward pause.

"Well, I won't keep you," she finally says. "I'll text you the details to the shower. Just let me know if you're coming. Maybe you could bring a new friend!"

Right. Because Nat would definitely want to take time off work to go to a baby shower. The alternative is even funnier. I can't even imagine what Oliver would look like surrounded by pink bows and baby onesies.

"Alright mom. Love you."

"Love you too, baby."

She hangs up and the phone goes silent.

I tuck it back in with my clothes and lay down on my back. Beth hasn't tried calling me back, or texting me. It's possible I burnt that bridge for good. Probably for the better. Maybe I'll just push away everyone who's ever cared about me and then I won't have to worry.

Stupid. Stupid Stella.

I get out the journal and write down two more points.

5. Stop thinking about Leo. It's in the past.

6. Figure out how not to push everyone away (good luck)

I then stuff it back into my clothes and walk straight for the ocean, ignoring all of the people around me. Normally, I love to people watch. Not today. Today, I want to pretend I'm the only person alive.

I swim until I am pruning and my limbs are tired. The waves aren't too bad today, but still take more effort to push through than any lakes at home.

When I get out, the air is beginning to cool off and most beach goers have left for dinner, leaving me almost completely alone on a beautiful beach.

I say almost because besides a few towels still scattered about with families, there is also a very tired looking Oliver leaning up against the side of a house. People are leaving the sidewalk and circling down around to go inside. The house is blue with a wrap around porch and brown shutters.

Oliver's head is leaned back and I think his eyes are closed. He's ignoring every person that walks by him as if they aren't even there.

Without thinking, I dry off my body and yank on my skirt and tank top. They immediately get wet, but I ignore it, moving the towel to patting down my hair instead. When the frizzy mess is at least half dry, I twist it up into a messy bun and wrap the journal and my phone into the now damp towel.

My feet are dirty with sand when I reach Oliver.

"Not going into your own party?" I ask.

His eyes pop open and a tired smile rests on his lips.

"Caleb's party."

"Your house though."

"Our house," He chuckles. "I will go in."

"Long day?"

"Work was rough."

My eyebrows draw together and I plop down onto the sand under the porch. Oliver looks at me for a moment before joining me. He isn't wet, so the sand doesn't cling to his legs like it does mine.

He brushes a patch of sand from my calf and I shiver.

"Where do you work?"

He's quiet for a moment, focusing on cleaning the sand from my leg before he answers. I wish I could roll around in the stuff without it looking weird so he would never stop touching me.

"A crisis center."

"That must be really rough."

"It is," he nods, his hand leaving me to run through his hair instead. "Some days the good outweighs the bad, you know? You help someone and it makes all of the bad stuff go away. But today was not one of those days."

"Do you want a small break?"

"All the time."

"Do you like baby showers?"

"Huh?"

Fuck. When will I learn to think before I speak? Either I think too much or I don't think enough. Maybe I should add that to the journal.

"My sister in law is having a baby shower next week that I don't want to go to."

"So you want me to go?"

"We are friends, right?" I laugh, using his words against him.

"Friends go to their friends' families' baby showers, is that what you're telling me?"

"Think of it as a vacation." I say. "It would only be a few days. Don't feel obligated or anything, I was really only joking anyway."

"You don't need to do that around me."

"Do what?"

"Pretend. Lie. Back track. I would love to go to a baby shower with you. I'll see if I can get it off work tomorrow. Just text me the days."

What? Did I really just ask Oliver, hot guy, totally emotionally available and apparently into me, Oliver, to go to Malory's baby shower with me? And did he say yes? "Oh…okay."

He smiles and stands up, offering a hand down to me. I take it and he gently pulls me up.

"Ready to go into the party?"

"Not really." I say honestly.

"Best thing about parties at my own house," He says. "If they get lame or overwhelming, there's a lock on my bedroom door."

I know he means to get away from the noise, but the word lock and bedroom in the same sentence coming out of Oliver's mouth does things to me I haven't felt in a long time.

I can feel my face flushing deep red, so I duck, wishing my hair was still down so it could hide my face. Oliver only chuckles, not letting go of my hand as he toes me inside.

Chapter Six

"Tell her about the one Caleb dared you to get!" Nat is shit faced drunk, leaning over me on the couch to point a finger at Oliver, who she's been forcing to tell me about every one of his tattoos for twenty minutes.

"Oh, now that's a good one." Caleb laughs from where he's laying on the floor. That stupid, tattered old hat is laying on his chest - someone should really buy him a new one. A girl with a short pixie cut is lying next to him, and they are both also very drunk.

I myself haven't drank a drop. Neither has Oliver that I have noticed.

I haven't drank since freshman year of college. Never again will I allow myself to get that vulnerable and exposed. Drunk people are unpredictable. I can't be unpredictable. I can't lose control.

"Let me see!" I laugh. It's easier to talk to people when you know they are intoxicated and if you say anything stupid, they probably won't remember in the morning.

"It's not my favorite," Oliver groans, laying his head back on the couch.

He's so close, our bodies are pressed tightly together. Nat is pressed up against my other side, but that side isn't tingling the way my right is.

"Come on," I poke him in the ribs.

"Fine. For you," he groans, untangling himself from the vacuum that is the couch and standing to his feet. I giggle, watching him pull at the side of his shirt to reveal a tattoo covered stomach and back. Ten minutes ago when he lifted his shirt to show off a snake starting at his shoulder and winding down to his pantline, my heart just about stopped and my hands turned sweaty. This time, my body has a milder reaction, but I still bite down on my lip as he points it out.

"Is that a Unicorn?" The moment the image on his left hip becomes clear among all of the other pictures it sits in, I jump up, a hand over my mouth.

Caleb is in a fit of laughter on the floor and Nat is rolling around on the couch with a fist pressed to her mouth.

"Tell the story, Olly, I can't!" She screams hysterically. I glance around at the rest of the party, but no one seems to be paying attention to us. The house is packed with bodies. It's a two story house and has quite a bit of space, but most of the bodies are crammed into this basement area. Still no one seems to even be looking in our direction, despite how loud Caleb and Nat are being.

"It is indeed a Unicorn," Oliver sighs. He puts his shirt down much to my dismay. You could wash laundry on those abs. "It was one of the first ones I got actually. I was fifteen-"

"Fifteen?!" I interrupt. "I thought you had to be sixteen to get a tattoo."

"You do," Oliver laughs. "Caleb's dad has a shop and he did them under the table for us as long as they could be hidden. So we were at Caleb's one night playing truth or dare. I dared Nat to go upstairs and confess her undying love to Caleb's father. Caleb had the biggest crush on Nat at the time so he got mad at me and dared me to get a unicorn tattoo. He didn't think I'd actually do it."

"Oh my God," I collapse back onto the couch next to Nat in a fit of laughter.

Sitting up straight, Nat's hands fly to her face and her lips pop into an O.

"I have the best idea."

"That is never a good thing," Oliver laughs, crossing his arms over his chest.

"Oh, shut up." She waves a hand at him and then grabs my hands and holds them tight against her chest. "Stella, you should get a tattoo. Tonight!"

"Nat, that's not-" Oliver starts but whether it is the high of seeing everyone else so happy or if I have actually lost my mind, I interrupt him.

"Let's do it."

"What?" Caleb sits up straight and asks the question at the same time as Oliver. "Do you have any?"

I shake my head.

"No," I look up at Oliver who is still standing with his arms crossed, but his expression has changed. He is looking at me with awe. "You'll come, right?"

He nods.

"Of course."

Within minutes we are a laughing mess of a group, staggering up the sidewalk with Caleb in the lead. The pixie cut girl tagged along, her arm looped with Caleb's. They all insisted it was only a few minutes away, and neither Nat or Caleb were really capable of being in a car right now anyway.

Aunt Milly is sitting on the front porch when we walk by, and her gaze follows us. I smile and give her a small wave which she doesn't return. I can't tell if she's mad or upset, or maybe in the dark she doesn't recognize me. Either way, I look back slightly less elated.

"Nat told me your Aunt doesn't approve." Oliver leans down to whisper in my ear so only I can hear. His voice is deep and gravely and when he whispers, shivers go down my spine.

"She doesn't."

He doesn't say anything else, or try to elaborate on why she may not. Instead, he straightens back up and keeps his gaze ahead.

When we reach the tattoo shop, nerves have begun to set in. Impulsively getting a tattoo is stupid right? But it's also not something old Stella would ever have done. This is new Stella. This is drop out, less than perfect Stella. And this Stella really wants to do this.

That doesn't mean I'm not about ready to bite off my fingernails completely with the nerves coursing through my body right now.

The lights are off in the shop, but Caleb reaches into his pocket and fumbles out a key. By the time he's gotten it in the door, a light has flipped on inside and a burly man with a long beard is getting ready to open the door.

"Hey guys," he laughs as Caleb stumbles in and the rest of us follow.

"Hey dad," Caleb throws himself into a reclining chair and the pixie cut girl sits on his lap. "Stella wants to get her first tattoo. Tattoo virgin."

I gulp and give a tiny wave.

"That's me."

The man turns towards me and I fight off the urge to stagger backwards. Oliver's hand curls around mine and squeezes and my breathing settles.

"Nice to meet you. I'm Tom, Caleb's dad. What did you want to get?"

"Do you have time now?" Oliver asks, shooting his best friend a glare for being so rude. Oliver spins the ball cap on Caleb's head to the side which awards him the middle finger and a tongue sticking out. Other than that, Caleb merely shrugs at the comment, entirely unphased.

"Yeah, if it's small. I was just finishing up some paperwork. Thank you for asking though, Olly," he shoots his son the same glare to which Caleb shrugs again.

There is a wall of small tattoo examples behind the seat Caleb is sitting in. I step closer to it, dragging Oliver with me. He stays close and I welcome it.

"That one." I point to a tiny outline of a heart. It's simple and cute and hopefully not too painful.

"I get to pick where you get it!" Nat screams.

"Within reason," I tell her.

She twists her lips around and narrows her eyes, scanning my body for several long moments before she nods, happy with her decision.

She leans over to Tom and whispers in his ear. He looks over at me.

"She says your hip."

My face flushes deep red. Nat's eyes are daring me. Caleb is assessing me. Oliver hasn't moved and I can't see his face. Which means he can't see the shade of red I just turned. Good.

"Okay." I say.

Everyone looks surprised, including myself, I am sure. I ignore that as Tom starts for the back room and begins to get his needle set up. He's showing me the unopened packages and their expiration numbers through the curtain, but I haven't moved.

I can't go in there alone, but I also can't bring this whole crew with me. With all my luck, Caleb or Nat would knock the needle out of Tom's hand. They are both too drunk to be in there.

"Come in with me?" I ask Oliver, still with my back turned to him.

He grabs my arm with the hand not holding mine and gently spins me around to face him. He's smiling, a wide grin that stretches from one side of his face to the other. What is making him so happy? I'm not sure, but whatever it is, I want to keep making it happen.

"Of course," he nudges me in the direction of the room where Tom is ready, waiting for me.

I tug the sheer curtain shut. It blurs what is happening on the other side but does nothing to block out their loud chatter and laughter.

Thank God I was at the beach before the party. I simply tug the skirt off and hop up on the bed Tom has ready for me. Laying on my back, the panic begins to set in at the most opportune time, just as Tom is about to start working the needle over my skin.

"Um, wait a minute," I tell him, my breathing beginning to quicken.

"Everything okay?" Tom asks.

I nod.

Oliver's head bends down into my vision and then he's pulling a chair up next to me and his hand is finding mine.

"You don't have to do this, Stella. Nat will get over it if you don't."

"I want to."

"Okay," he says, squeezing my hand. "What can I do to help?"

I wish I knew.

"Don't leave."

Don't leave like everyone else always does. Don't give up on me like everyone always does. Also, just don't leave me alone in this tattoo shop.

"I won't." He whispers.

"Ready when you are," Tom says.

I nod, feeling his hand rest on the side of my hip bone. He's placed the stencil just above my bikini strap. I know from watching movies that usually the artist asks you if you like the placement before they start. But I don't care.

"Happy thoughts." He mutters, and then a pain like intense cat scratches pounds into my hip bone.

I squeeze my eyes closed and tighten my grip on Oliver's hand. He scoots closer and his entire arm presses against my side.

"Not too bad right?" He asks.

"Not too bad." I agree. As the vibrations continue, I open my eyes, and he's right. The pain isn't too bad, once you get used to it. It's the dragging feeling of the needle over my skin that is bugging me out.

I turn my head over to find Oliver's face inches from mine. When our eyes lock, I expect him to look away. But he doesn't.

Chapter Seven

"Let's go to the beach." Aunt Milly flips a pancake in the pan, flashing a smile over her shoulder at me.

My stomach flips. Do I tell her about the tattoo? If we're going to the beach, I don't really have a choice.

"Okay," I say, trying to sound enthusiastic. "By the way, what would you say if I told you I got a tattoo?" I force the words out as quickly as I can.

Aunt Milly slides the pancake from the pan onto the stack beside her and shuts off the burner before turning around. When she does, a surprising smile is filling her face. She tugs down the waistband of her pajama pants to show me a small seashell on her hip bone.

My mouth pops open.

"No way." I breathe.

"This is my first. I got it the year I moved here. Your Gram always wanted to get one and never got to. So I did it for her."

"You have more?"

She laughs and grabs the plate, bringing it to the table and sitting it beside the butter and maple syrup I have already set up with our plates.

"There are some things about your Aunt you don't know, Stella."

"I guess so." I say, helping myself to a pancake. This is our first day off together since I got here.

I was able to get three days off for the baby shower next week. My boss, Dan, is pretty understanding and was willing to give me the entire week. I don't think I can take that much time with my family. Aunt Milly won't make it. Her boutique needs her too much. I haven't talked to Oliver since two nights ago at the tattoo shop. He probably forgot about agreeing to go with me anyway.

It's not a big deal.

"So," she wiggles her eyebrows. "Where did you get your first?"

I stand and show her the heart, shiny from the ointment I've been applying as often as possible. It's not raised anymore and barely red. Tom wouldn't let me pay, but I did slide him a twenty as a tip as we left the shop. He clapped me on the shoulder and thanked me, laughing about how none of Caleb's friends ever pay.

"I went with Nat two nights ago," I tell her, conveniently leaving out the others in the party. It's no use though, she sees right through my bullshit.

"You don't have to lie to me, honey. I saw you with Oliver and Caleb too. I'm not mad."

"You're not?"

"I simply meant to be careful. I trust that you are."

I distract myself by stuffing a bite of pancake into my mouth. Aunt Milly's kind eyes are locked on mine. Sometimes, I swear it's like she can see right through your soul.

"I love the tattoo. It's perfect." She says. "I have something I want to show you, when you're finished eating."

Her cryptic offer sends shivers of excitement down my spine as I begin to scarf my food down. Any insight into my Aunt's past is not only welcomed but overwhelmingly exciting. Despite her living next to us in Vermont for most of my upbringing, I don't know much about my Aunt. Mom never wants to talk about her, leaving her entire life story a bit of a mystery. I've never had the courage to ask.

Once we've both washed off our plates, Aunt Milly leads me down the hallway to the basement stairs. We descend into the dusty stairwell lit by a single light that flickers, hanging from the ceiling.

The basement is full of boxes stacked to the ceiling. There is only a single path running down the center, which I follow her down until we are in the very back of the large room.

"Most of this stuff belonged to your Grandmother. Some of it I brought with me seven years ago and haven't touched since. I need to go through it all. In time." Aunt Milly muses, her voice soft and gentle as she picks a large brown box from a stack and hefts it down to the floor.

"I had no idea so much was down here." I say, sinking down onto my knees beside her as she begins to peel off the tape holding the box shut.

"This house, this family - we have more than our share of baggage, Stella. Not all of it can be packed away into boxes."

She grabs a brown scrapbook from the top and pushes the box aside, leaning against it. The book in her hands is dusty and worn. It looks like it came from another time. As she opens it, the spine groans and the pages crinkle.

"Here." She hands it to me, a tired smile on her lips. I grab the book and gently rest it on my knee.

The first page is labeled 1994 and has a single polaroid photo taped to it. It's grainy and the photo is dark, but it's a picture of a boy. He looks young, maybe a junior or senior in High School. It's only his profile and he's looking out over a mountain at the trees below, a handsome smile on his face.

"Who's this?" I ask.

"I loved him," she answers with a shrug. "It wasn't enough."

"Don't they say if you love something you shouldn't give up on it?" I ask. This is from so long ago, maybe she doesn't even remember the boy's name. But he looks so happy. She must have been too to keep his photo all of these years.

Scribbled beside the photo is a little black heart with T + M written beside it.

"I gave up on love a long time ago, Stella," She sighs. "It's not a sad thing. It's life."

I swallow hard and decide to flip to the next page instead of lingering on her words. I can't imagine loving someone that much and simply giving up.

The next page is labeled 1998, San Jose California. Another polaroid photo is taped to the page, this one of Aunt Milly. She looks so young and vibrant, her long hair braided into pigtails. She's wearing a tube top and long skirt, smiling wide as she stands in front of a camper van.

"What were you doing in California?"

She reaches forward and flips to the next page for me. This one reads 1998 Tucson Arizona. The photo is of a single cactus.

"Like I said Stell-Bells, there's things you don't know about your Aunt. Just don't be so quick to think I'd judge you, honey. I've seen my share of the world and I've done my share of crazy things. I'm only ever looking out for you. I hope you understand that."

I nod and she smiles, reaching forward and taking the book before I can flip to the next page. She quietly sticks it back into the box and before we leave the basement, she stacks two other boxes on top of it, signaling that I'm not welcome to come down and look through it farther.

I won't. Somehow, though I want to know everything there is to know about Aunt Milly's past, I also know it's none of my business until she chooses to share it with me.

We do end up going to the beach. It's cloudy today, so it's not as packed as usual. I avoid the water and keep my shirt on when laying in the partial sun. While Aunt Milly is out in the water, I take out the journal and stare at the first page.

I don't have any more things to add to the list right now, so I flip to the next page.

Things I've Done in Maine

I make the heading and then begin to list them underneath. Got a job, met a cute boy, got a tattoo. I underline cute boy as if there's a chance I'd forget about him. I picture myself years from now brushing through these pages and reliving each moment. I wonder if Aunt Milly ever did the same thing with her polaroid photos of the handsome boy from 1994.

I imagine myself in my forties reminiscing over these pages, remembering the boy I spent so much time with that one summer. There is no way I wouldn't even then still have Oliver's beautiful green eyes seared into my brain.

*   *   *

I texted Oliver the details for the baby shower last week and he never answered. He hasn't been by the diner. Nat and Caleb don't seem to know anything either. Caleb asks why I don't just walk over to their house and ask him in person, to which I shake my head and leave the conversation.

It's not a big deal. I am fully capable of going to see my family on my own. Really, who had I thought I was, asking him to come along? I don't even know him and he doesn't know me. He probably thought it was odd and has decided to shut me off completely.

I wouldn't blame him.

I'm loading my duffel bag into the backseat of my car when I see him leaving his house across the street.

He has a backpack slung over his shoulder and is walking straight towards me.

Thankfully Aunt Milly is at work, because I never told her I'd asked Oliver to come and it's not something I really want to talk about right now. I bite down on my lip and watch as Oliver crosses the street.

He looks tired, but he's smiling. I love the way he walks. It's so confident, with his shoulders back. He takes long strides, his hair bouncing softly on his shoulders. He's wearing his signature cargo shorts and a soft blue t-shirt.

"Hey." He says as he approaches me. "Don't leave without me." He chuckles.

"I was starting to think you weren't coming."

"Why would you think that? I said I would."

"Right. But then you haven't talked to me since."

His brows knit together as he throws his bag into the trunk with my duffel. When he turns back to me, he cocks his head to the side.

"I'll always do what I say I'm going to do, Stella. I promise."

"I thought maybe you were…"

"I was what?"

Damnit. I'm lost in his eyes again. My tongue is tied and I'm not even sure where I was going. Taking a deep breath, I shrug and pretend I didn't even start shoving my foot in my mouth, hoping he'll follow along. I walk around the car and slide into the passenger seat.

"The crisis center got really busy this week," Oliver slides in next to me and closes the door. "You are welcome at our place, if I'm ever not answering or-"

"No, you don't have to explain yourself." I cut him off, flushing deep red as I turn the car on.

Oliver's hand grabs mine as I turn the key, snapping my attention to him.

"I don't mind. If it helps you."

Is it possible to get so red your face actually burns off? Because if it is, I think it might happen to me.

"Okay." I say. He seems to accept that, because his hand leaves mine and we fall into comfortable silence.

Using my GPS, I guide us out of Bar Harbor and find the Highway. I like driving. I always have. It clears my head and gives me something else to focus on that isn't my thoughts. The drive from Aunt Milly's to my parents is roughly five hours. It's a long drive, but it's one I rather enjoy. Especially in the summer with the windows cracked as they are now, a light breeze blowing through my hair.

Oliver has taken a book out of his pocket, and this time, it isn't his journal. It's an actual book with the spine bent and cover worn. He's reading as I drive. As much as I want to know what the book is, I don't want to interrupt his calm, so I keep my mouth closed.

We stop twice to use the bathroom at random rest stops, also grabbing drinks and snacks.

"Do you want me to take a turn at the wheel?" Oliver asks at the first rest stop, resting his hands on the top of the car as he waits for me to answer. I shake my head.

"Thanks, but no," I slide back into the driver's seat and turn the key in the ignition, all before he's slid in beside me. With the click of his seatbelt, I begin back onto the road. "Maybe you can drive the way back. I like driving."

"Deal." He nods, his fingers playing with his book in his lap. For a moment, I think he's going to pick it back up again. We've been in the car about an hour and have spoken very little, which I actually don't mind. But are we going to spend the entire car ride this way? "Tell me about your family." He finally says. His fingers leave the book's spine and rest on his legs instead.

"What? Why?"

"I am about to meet them," he smiles, shrugging. "Am I walking into a lion's den or more like a dog kennel?"

I think he's making a joke, but I don't laugh because I'm too busy actually contemplating the answer. My family is complicated. Of course we love each other, but you wouldn't know it at first glance. So maybe a bit closer to a lion's den.

"My mom, Elanor, can be a lot. Most people don't believe her and Aunt Milly are even sisters at first. She's very driven. And very opinionated."

"And your dad?"

"Simon." I take a deep breath, deciding how to describe my dad. "He's quiet. He lets mom do her thing and kind of just rides the waves. It's always been that way. Sometimes I wish he cared a bit more. When Aunt Milly lived in Vermont still, things were easier. She was like the big sister I never had. Old enough to be my mom but carefree enough to be a sister."

"What about your actual siblings?"

"Daven is cool. He's your typical brother. A pain in the ass but he'd do anything for me. Elsie is an overachiever. She's mom's perfect golden child. I love her to pieces but sometimes I think mom pushes her too hard to be who she wishes she'd been."

Why am I saying so much? I should shut up, but he looks so intrigued and he's not telling me to. I veer into the passing lane and press the gas a bit harder, passing a van doing ten under the speed limit. The driver yawns and glances over at us.

"Enough about me," I say before he has a chance to answer. "Is your family more like a lion's den too?"

Oliver's face drops slightly. It's such a small change, at first I think I've imagined it. Until he answers, and his voice is off too.

"My parents were never completely in the picture," he says and I feel my heart drop. "They never wanted a kid so I was more of a burden to them than anything else. Honestly I spent more time at Caleb and Chris's from the time I was nine until the time I moved out than I did at my own home."

"I'm sorry. My parents may irritate me but at least I always knew they loved me. I can't imagine," I say, trying not to get too emotional.

Family has always been everything to me. Whether it was my parents, my siblings, or Aunt Milly, I always knew I had someone to fall back on.

"I had Tom," Oliver shrugs, a small smile sliding back onto his lips. "Caleb's dad couldn't have been a better role model. He taught me basically everything I needed to know. Even when Caleb turned 18 and inherited the beach house and moved out, I still spent most of my time at Tom's. I was never alone. So don't feel too bad for me."

He winks and his smile widens.

The topic shifts to something more lighthearted. I talk about my childhood home and he talks about growing up on the ocean. We discuss our favorite books and TV shows, all while scenery passes by in the blur.

I haven't even noticed how much time has passed until a lull hits our conversation about the best hiking spots in Vermont, and Oliver clears his throat.

"Want to play a game?" He asks me. The GPS is reading about one more hour left of our drive. We are both getting sick of sitting still, though this is the quickest this drive has ever passed for me. Oliver's voice is soothing as I navigate us into less condensed traffic.

"Sure."

"Would you rather?"

"You go first."

"Naturally," He rubs his palms together, narrowing his eyes. "Alright. Would you rather save the world, but you get no credit for it, or let the world go up in flames?"

Laughter shakes my body.

"Hard hitter starter question. Easy though. Definitely let the world go up in flames."

"Really?"

"No! Not really. Of course I'd save the world."

His laughter is intoxicating.

"You had me worried for a second. Your turn."

I tap my chin as I rack my brain for something funny to ask him.

"Alright. I got one. Would you rather fight one bear sized duck, or one hundred duck sized bears?"

It's his laughter that fills the car this time. I find myself having to keep myself from doubling over with my own laughter just from the sound of his. It's contagious. Oliver doesn't just laugh once. When he laughs, his entire body shakes, his head tosses back, his arms cross over his chest or smack his knees.

"Okay," he sobers up. "I've gotta go with one hundred duck sized bears. Right? I could just like, kick them or something."

"What if they bite you?"

"But a giant duck could just swallow me whole!"

"You've got a point."

"Okay, okay. My turn."

Our game continues until I am pulling into my brother's driveway. I park the car next to Daven's minivan and cut the engine, wiping a hand across my cheek as tears of laughter fall there.

"Come on. You are seriously telling me you would rather have no elbows than no knees?" He asks. "How would you write or shake someone's hand?"

"But with no knees you can't walk!"

Daven is walking out of the house, waving, with Malory two steps behind him. They are an odd couple, but somehow, it works for them. Daven is short like me with the same blonde hair, only his is in a buzzcut. He's got round glasses and wears only polo shirts with black jeans. Malory is a good head taller than him with hair dyed bright purple today. The last time I saw her, it was pink. She's seven months pregnant, her belly adorable under the bright red sundress she's wearing.

I hop out of the car and run straight for Daven. I've missed him. When I dropped out of college, I drove straight to mom's house. When she broke the news that her spare room wasn't available, it was only hours later that I was packing up and getting on the road for Aunt Milly's. Daven, although he only lives a short drive from mom and dad, was at work at the time. He tried convincing me to go to his place over the phone, but he's much easier to ignore when you don't have to look into that round face.

"Dude, you act like it's been years," Daven laughs as I pull back from giving him a bear hug.

"Months Daven. Might as well be years." I turn to Malory and pull her in next. "You look so good, Mal."

"We're glad you could make it." Malory pulls back. "I didn't think your mom was going to let me be involved in the planning at first. I think I'm a bit too weird for her sometimes."

I laugh, because it's true.

"Mom can be a saint, Malory, you know that. But she is also stuck in her ways. You'll break through her shell one day, I promise."

"I've been trying for years," Malory laughs, and then her eyes cut sideways and I notice Oliver has walked up beside me. "Who's this?"

An awkward introduction, one of many, commences. They continue as we walk inside and my little sister, Elsie, is sitting on the couch. And again when my parents arrive. Everyone wants to know who Oliver is and why he is here.

"I'm a friend," Oliver explains to mom and dad for the last time as he shakes their hands. "I'm a big fan of baby showers."

That elicits a round of laughter, but I know I'm not off the hook. Mom keeps looking at me out of the corner of her eye. She's going to attack me with questions the moment we are alone.

Which is exactly why I make it a point to not make myself alone.

I succeed all through dinner and well into the evening. It's only when Daven tugs Oliver into the living room to show him his movie collection and dad follows, that Mom is able to sidle up next to me at the kitchen counter before I can scoot off too.

"So, how is Aunt Milly's?"

"Good. It's really good."

"I can see that." Malory laughs, clearly talking about Oliver. I blush deep red.

"He really is just a friend. I've only been in Maine a little over a week. He couldn't possibly be more yet if I wanted him to."

Shit. Shouldn't have said that.

"Your dad and I were engaged in two months, Stella. You can't lie to me." Mom puts her hands on her hips.

"No one is getting engaged."

"Does your Aunt approve?"

I gulp. Fuck.

"There isn't anything to approve of because we aren't dating, mom. I can be friends with whoever I want."

Mom's eyes narrow.

"So that's a no?"

I shrug and pounce on Elsie who has just entered the room. She's used to being used as a distraction, so she comes easily when I tug her into the bathroom going off about how I need help fixing my hair. Since my hair is a hot mess on top of my head, everyone knows it's a lie, but no one says anything.

As the evening comes to an end, Mom, dad and Elsie leave. Malory is tired, so she gives both Oliver and I a hug and putters off to bed. The shower is tomorrow. We are only here for two nights and oddly enough, I am already glad I invited Oliver. My family can be tough for me to be around. They mean well, but they don't always come across that way. At least with Oliver here, my crippling failures and terrible mental health aren't the highlight of conversations. Oliver is.

I'll take the embarrassment over the sadness any day.

"Sorry," Daven points to the stairs. "I didn't know you were bringing anyone so we just have the guest room set up. I can grab some blankets for the couch if you want."

"I've got it, Daven. Go be with your pregnant wife," I punch him on the shoulder.

"Alright. Goodnight."

Alone in the kitchen, the silence between Oliver and I is suddenly awkward with this new information looming between us.

"I can sleep on the couch," He offers.

"I invited you. I'm not going to make you sleep on a hard couch."

"Well I'm not gonna allow you too either."

I narrow my eyes.

"We're in a standoff then."

He laughs.

I hope he can't hear my heart beating out of my chest. My mind is racing and my palms are sweating, which are usually signs that a panic attack is about to take over. But I feel fine. My breathing isn't coming faster, my vision isn't blurring. I'm fine. Odd.

Without saying another word, I start up the stairs for the guest bedroom. I know Oliver is following me, but I refuse to turn back and look.

The guest room is small and familiar. I've stayed here many times on vacations home from college. For some reason, my brother's house has felt safer than my parents has for quite some time.

I sit my duffel down at the end of the bed and Oliver sits his backpack next to it.

I don't even realize I'm staring at him until he clears his throat. What is it he sees on my face? His own looks concerned, his brow wrinkled.

"Stella, are you okay?"

I nod.

"I'm um…" I wring my hands out. What am I?

"Stella, I don't want you to think I have any expectations here. I really did come as a friend."

"Right."

So that's all he sees me as.

"Just friends?"

His eyes search mine again. Should I say being just friends with him is the last thing I want? Do I say that since the moment I saw him I've wanted to kiss him? If I was anyone else, maybe I would.

But I don't.

And the moment is over.

"Just friends." He nods, a small smile on his lips. Do I detect regret in his eyes too? No. I must be imagining it. I force a smile onto my own lips.

"Then we can share this bed, right?"

"Are you sure?"

My mouth is dry, but I nod.

"I mean, we're just friends. So why not?"

He doesn't answer, and I can't take the humiliation anymore, so I grab my bag and shut myself in the bathroom. My reflection in the mirror mocks me. He had said he wanted to be around me; had I read too much into that? He also said he wanted to be friends that night on the cliff edge.

I wash my face, brush my teeth, and change into shorts and a baggy t-shirt. Gathering all of the courage I can, I walk back out into the room with my shoulders back and head held high.

Oliver is laying on top of the covers.

I crawl underneath them next to him and roll over, closing my eyes.

In silence, he goes to the bathroom himself. He's gone for a while and when he comes back, he shuts off the light and climbs into bed beside me. He also gets under the covers and my breath hitches.

What is he wearing? Is he wearing a shirt?

"Stella?" He whispers into the dark.

Should I pretend I am sleeping? That seems a bit juvenile. I assess the situation quickly, as I've learned to do when my anxiety is taking over.

There is no threat I can perceive here. Oliver is laying in bed next to me, but he is not touching me. We are friends. Friends can share a bed. So why do I suddenly want to be kissing him?

I shift.

"Yeah?"

"Would you rather have a head the size of a tennis ball or a watermelon?"

I burst out laughing, filling the silence as Oliver's own shakes the bed.

"I guess tennis ball. Can you imagine how heavy a watermelon head would be?"

"But how is anyone supposed to kiss a tennis ball head?"

My breath hitches. Is he thinking about kissing me too then? Or is he just continuing on with the joke?

As our laughter wanes, silence takes over the darkness again. I take in a deep breath.

"Oliver."

"Hm?"

"Would you rather be able to change one event in your past or be able to see one event in the future?"

My breath hitches. I know exactly what my answer would be. Changing one event in my past would make everything now so much different. Although there are so many moments I would want to change, I'm not sure where I would even start.

He is quiet for a long moment.

"Neither. Can I choose neither?"

I roll onto my back and stare up at the dark ceiling. The streetlights outside are casting a thin beam of light across the bed, illuminating a strip of the comforter.

"Why neither?"

"I hate some things that happened in my past," He says, his voice quiet. "But I wouldn't change any of it. That could fuck up where I am now. And I don't want to know what's going to happen in the future. That ruins it."

"Ruins it?"

"Do you like rollercoasters, Stella?"

"I do."

"My first therapist when I was fifteen explained life to me like a rollercoaster. He said there are so many twists and turns and drops, and sometimes you're scared, not knowing what is going to come next, but when you get off, you almost always want to go again."

"How are you so mentally stable?" I laugh.

"Trust me," He chuckles, a low sound. "If you knew what was going on in my head half the time, you wouldn't be saying that."

"Like what?"

"Like how badly I want to kiss you right now. Or how badly I've wanted to kiss you since the moment I met you."

Chapter Eight

"Okay, but Stella, you can't just ignore him. You are going to have to drive five hours with him tomorrow, or did you forget?" It is the next day, and I am hiding in the downstairs bathroom on the pretense of taking a very long shower while Malory sits on the side of the tub, trying to talk some sense into me.

I bury my head in my hands.

Last night, after Oliver said quite possibly the hottest thing I have ever heard come out of anyone's mouth, I pretended to be asleep. Surely, he didn't buy it, as I had just spoken. But I didn't know what else to do.

I panicked, and I pretended to be sleeping.

Now, having slipped from the room before he woke up, I have no idea what to do. So as Malory was puttering around getting ready for the baby shower, I pushed her into the bathroom with me so I could talk to someone who isn't insane.

"What if I just leave now and leave him money for a bus ticket?"

"Stella," Mallory grabs my hands and forces my face up so I have no choice but to look into her eyes. "Do you like him?"

I nod.

"So what is the problem?"

Before I can answer, her eyes grow soft and realization dawns across her features.

"Leo?"

"Partially." I say, because yeah, what happened with Leo isn't helping. But that's not entirely it. I feel safe with Oliver. "What if I'm just too broken, Mal?" I finally whisper, forcing the tears back as I hear my voice break.

Malory smiles, a tiny smile, and then nods.

"Okay, this is what we're going to do. I need you to come with me to town and run errands before the party. I'll tell Daven to occupy Oliver this morning. It'll give you some time to think before you see him this afternoon."

Genius. Sure, it's the coward's way out. But at this moment, I am totally fine with being a coward.

So Malory and I do exactly that. I push Oliver to the back of my mind, and force myself to have fun with Malory as we walk around the mall. We don't do many errands, instead pop in and out of stores, trying on random outfits and silly hats.

I forgot how much I loved spending time with Malory. She is the best thing that has ever happened for Daven, and I am ecstatic she is part of our family.

As soon as that thought pops into my head, I shove it out because it makes me feel instantly guilty.

I moved away from my family on a whim simply because I didn't feel good enough. I completely forgot about Malory and how included she has always made me feel. I wonder if she was mad at me when I just took off without giving her and Daven a second thought.

The baby shower is at the small town hall in my hometown. When we arrive, the parking lot is already jam-packed full of cars, Daven's parked right out front. Which means Oliver is inside.

Malory walks ahead, her shoulders back.

This isn't about me anymore and I am now on my own. Good thing baby showers are full of family and people I haven't seen in a long time.

I'm able to spend most of the time avoiding Oliver, who by the look on his face, knows exactly what I am doing. It doesn't help that he looks better than usual today. He's wearing a button down white top and jeans. I haven't seen him in anything other than cargo shorts. His hair is down and five o'clock shadow runs across his chin. The fact that he keeps looking for me in the crowded room is sending butterflies into my stomach. I feel like I might throw up.

"Aunt Milly says she didn't know you were bringing Oliver," my mom sidles up next to me as I shove a hot pink cupcake in my mouth.

I nearly choke.

"Mom," I finally say, wiping the crumbs from my lips before responding. "It's really not a big deal."

"Uh-huh. Anyway, boy drama aside, do you think moving to Maine for the summer was a good choice? What are your thoughts now on college next year?"

Of course those two things would connect in her brain.

"I'm not going back to college, mom."

"But you were so close to graduating, sweetie," her tone is light, but her eyes are daggers. We've already had this conversation. She can't understand why someone would drop out at the end of their junior year. Honestly, if you had told me in High School that I would be that girl, I would have thought the same thing. I would have told you it didn't make any sense at all.

But having lived it, I can now say it doesn't make sense until you are actually living it.

Then it was the only choice that did make sense.

"Can we talk about something else?"

She sighs. I know she doesn't want to drop it. But she does, moving on to how things are going at the house with the guy renting out my room and my little sister. Apparently they had to implement some strict rules because the two were getting a bit too comfortable.

I'm laughing at mom's interpretation of Elsie fawning over the guy when Malory comes over and tugs her away to look at a pack of onesies she's amazed by.

Oliver is standing by the front door, looking incredibly calm and collected, and he is staring at me.

It's after three in the afternoon.

I asked the poor guy to come five hours away with me and I've spent the entire day ignoring him.

Feeling like an ass, I take a deep breath and walk towards him, grabbing a soda from the cooler as I go. I focus on opening it and taking a sip beside him before I say anything. He speaks first.

"Your family is nice."

Yeah, they are. Pushy, overbearing and a tad annoying, but they are nice. I don't want to talk about my family right now though, and I doubt he does either.

"I want to kiss you too," I whisper. "I want to do more than kiss you. I'm just not sure I am ready. I'm a mess, Oliver."

At first, I'm not sure he has heard me, as the silence stretches on. I am about to glance up at him from my soda can when his elbow bumps mine.

"Okay," He says. When I look up, he's smiling.

"You're not mad?"

"Mad? Stella," he lowers his voice and his head, bringing his lips to the side of my ear so that only I can hear him. His breath tickles my lobe, sending shivers down my spine. "I am a patient man. When you do trust me, because you will, our time spent together will only be made better because of the time it took to get there."

His words are innocent, but his voice is not.

I clamp down on my lower lip, feeling myself flush deep red. He is still leaning down. I press my hands into his chest and allow myself to lean against him.

"How are you so sure I am going to trust you?"

"Because I am a trustworthy guy," he chuckles. "And because I won't stop convincing you I deserve a shot until you give me one."

Chapter Nine

I am getting whiplash.

Our time spent in Vermont feels like it didn't even happen, as much as my time in Maine is beginning to feel like a dream.

We got back this morning. We left Daven's early so that Oliver could work a half shift at the center. They called him during the baby shower and asked if he could. I could tell he wanted to, so we left early to get sleep so we could wake up early.

Oliver drove the entire way and I napped while I wasn't doodling jumpy sketches in my journal. I have been finding myself writing in it more and more lately. I still haven't added to the original list on the first page, but I have drawn messy sketches and written oddly discombobulated poems.

It feels good.

My body is antsy from being in the car all day.

Aunt Milly is at work and I don't feel like being alone, so I take out my phone and call Nat.

She answers on the first ring and before I've even gotten a chance to change into a bathing suit and get to the front door, she's already knocking on it.

"I am so glad you called," she sighs as we walk across the street, past her tiny car and hordes of beach goers. It's a weekday, but the place is still packed. The weather is perfect today. It isn't too hot.

There is a breeze coming in off the ocean, but not a cold one. "I was going crazy sitting in my apartment. I am so nervous."

"For Carrie to come home?"

She'll be home in a week for their wedding in a little under two, and it's all Nat has been talking about. Our texts are full of Nat's rants about how the week will go and pictures of what outfits she should wear for each day.

She nods, laying her bright pink towel down in the sand.

I lay my own down next to her and strip my shorts and tank top off. The tattoo is mostly healed now, still slimy with ointment but not red or raised at all. I like the way it looks, just above my black bikini bottom. It's cute.

"I just haven't seen her in months, you know?"

"I am sure it will be great," I tell her. But I'm not sure. I don't even really know what I'm talking about. I hope it will be, for her sake.

"Anyway, enough about me. How was home?"

I sigh, laying on my stomach and letting my head fall into my hands. The sun is hot on my back and I welcome the heat, jogging me out of my thoughts.

"I am an idiot, is how it went."

She laughs.

"Why?"

Swallowing, I decide I am going to tell her. It's been a long time since I've had a friend to talk to like this. Beth and I used to confide everything in each other, but it's been years since that was the case. Even during college, the calls got less frequent as she moved in with her boyfriend and I struggled in school. We were going in different directions, and I felt like I couldn't connect with anyone. My therapist liked to say I was making it all up in my head, but I wasn't so sure that was the case.

Nat is easy to talk to.

And it doesn't feel like she is judging me.

"Oliver told me he wanted to kiss me."

Her mouth pops open.

"And you didn't jump his bones?"

Flushing deep red, I shake my head.

"No. Oliver is just…" I trail off, not sure where to find the words. "He's so whole. I am not that way. I just don't think I'd be good for him."

To my surprise, Nat laughs. She actually laughs.

"Stella, do me a favor and pull your head out of your ass," it sounds harsh, but her tone is light. "Oliver is far from whole. The guy is covered in tattoos, each dedicated to a different fucked up time in his life. He spends hours writing in a journal instead of talking to actual people. I love the guy, but he is so far from whole."

I want to ask her more.

I want her to divulge every secret she has on the guy. Instead, I just groan and sit up.

"I'm gonna swim."

She laughs.

"You do that. And while you're at it, consider the possibility that you're not the only broken human being alive!" She yells after me.

I stick my tongue out at her, but as I dive into the water, tears are threatening to spill down my cheeks. I ignore them, pushing through the water and letting my thoughts be washed away with each stroke.

Nat and I stay at the beach for most of the afternoon. We are sitting on our towels, people watching as the beach empties, when I realize I am staring at Oliver's house. And Oliver is walking inside.

"Let's go." Nat stands up, brushing sand off her legs. "I am starving."

"Where do you want to eat?" I yank my eyes away from Oliver's form disappearing inside. She hasn't noticed where I was staring, thankfully.

"Pizza?"

I agree, and we gather our things up, heading for Nat's car. She drives us to this tiny joint just outside of the hustle of the tourist town where they sell pizza by the slice. Our bodies tight and warm from the sun, we enjoy our pizza slices and soda, sitting across from each other.

"I think I like it here." I say after a big bite.

"Huh?" Nat pulls herself from her thoughts. "Were you expecting not to?"

"I think I convinced myself not to," I say. "I didn't want to like it."

"I'm sure Oliver is helping."

I glare at her and roll my eyes, but she isn't wrong, and she knows it. She giggles, taking a swig of her own drink.

"I'm glad you came. Now I just have to convince you not to leave."

I laugh, loudly.

"Yeah, right."

"What? Is that so ridiculous? What exactly do you have back home to go back to?"

"My family."

"Right. You also have family here."

I swallow hard and chew on the inside of my lip.

"I can't think that far ahead," I finally say. "I've only been here for like two weeks."

"People have made rasher decisions in less time. The year after I graduated High School, I got on a flight to Hawaii by myself with only five hundred dollars in my bank account. Quite possibly the stupidest thing I'll ever do, but I would do it again in a heartbeat."

"Tell me more about that story," I laugh.

Nat dives into a detailed story about her time in Hawaii, and I give her my full attention, forcing my thoughts to stay away from Oliver and how much I want to go see him.

*   *   *

I'm sitting on the deserted beach and it is pitch black out. I couldn't sleep, so at midnight, I snuck down across the road, wrapped in a blanket, and I've been sitting here for almost an hour. I'm staring up at the stars, getting a pretty nasty crick in my neck, when I hear footsteps padding through the sand towards me.

I know it is Oliver before I look over.

He sits down next to me and without thinking, I give him half of the blanket.

His body is warm, pressed up against mine.

"I have breakfast shift tomorrow," I say, my voice low and dry. "I should be sleeping."

"I have work at 7. I should be too."

"And yet neither of us are," I laugh quietly. "Can I ask you a personal question?"

"Always."

There are so many things I want to know. I decide to take the plunge. If I am going to go searching around in his past, I might as well start at the root of it.

"My Aunt warned me to stay away from you. Nat told me she should keep her opinions to herself. You haven't had much to say about it. Should I be worried? Like, are you a closet murderer or something?"

He doesn't laugh like I think he is going to.

My eyes widen and when he notices, he chuckles, but it isn't a noise filled with humor. It's low and dark.

"I guess you do deserve to know the whole truth about me. If we are going to fall in love and all that."

I laugh and this time he does too.

"Nobody said anything about love," I elbow him gently in the side, but the word sends tingles down my spine. Would I even know what love felt like if I was in it? I would hope so. I know what love feels like for family and friends. How long does it take for you to know you love someone? I definitely care about Oliver more than I've cared about even myself lately. I think about him more than I think about anything else.

But that doesn't mean I love him.

"You can have one truth tonight. Do you want the biggie from High School or the year after?"

"Hmm, only one?"

"For tonight, yeah."

"Okay. High School I guess."

I can't tell if that's the one he wanted me to pick or not. He takes a deep breath and lets it out.

"My best friend and Caleb's twin brother, Chris, committed suicide when we were all fifteen. When they searched his room, they found a letter I had written to him the week before. I was in an extremely dark place myself, and we'd made a sort of pact. If things didn't go the way we wanted by the end of the year…" he trailed off. "Well, let's just say we were going to go out together. When it got out to the public, which happened incredibly quickly, people blamed me for a long time."

I want to wrap my arms around him and pull him close to me. My heart feels like it is on fire. Could that possibly be what my Aunt is warning me about?

"That's terrible."

"After that," he continues, "Caleb and I started hanging out with some pretty bad crowds. We did things I'm not proud of the following year."

"Like?"

"Vandalism mostly. Drugs. If it weren't for Caleb's dad, Tom, we probably would have ended up behind bars before we were even old enough to know what life really was. Tom caught us before we really got off track and helped us back on. I owe him my life."

I swallow hard, picturing the rugged tattoo artist who drew the delicate heart on my hip. He is the reason Oliver is sitting next to me now, and even after his own son died. I can't imagine the strength.

"I am so sorry."

Oliver glances over at me.

"Your turn."

"My turn?"

"Well, I think it's only fair that I get one big thing too now. If you are comfortable."

"I'm not that interesting," I sigh. "But I guess you are right."

My struggles with depression and anxiety seem a bit too surface level with what he has just shared. He already knows about dropping out of college. He's already met my family.

I swallow hard.

"It's silly. Compared to what you just told me, it's really nothing but…" I trail off, finding my words. He doesn't interrupt me, so I continue. "My senior year of High School, this guy Leo and I were dating. He was the first guy I ever kissed. I thought I was in love with him. We were both running for valedictorian so we were on stage giving our speeches…I think he knew I was going to win and he never was good at losing…"

My voice fades off as I try to figure out how to explain what happened next.

"Leo was the kind of guy who could make anyone feel amazing. Just by touching you or talking to you, you'd feel like you were his whole world. He'd spent the night before telling me how beautiful my body was. And then, in front of the entire school, he made fun of me. He called me names, pointing out how chubby I looked in my skirt. I always loved the way I looked, and I still do, but until this past week, I hadn't worn a skirt since. And…. and I haven't kissed anyone since either. The idea of being that vulnerable ever again makes me feel sick."

The silence that follows is long, and I refuse to glance over to Oliver. I don't want to know what he is thinking.

"I know it's silly. It doesn't even compare to what you went through, but like I said I-"

Oliver is turning me towards him with his hands on my shoulders, the blanket falling off of us. The words are stolen from my mouth as he looks down at me, a fire lit in his eyes that could swallow me whole.

Before I can comprehend what is happening, his lips are lowering to mine. He pauses for a moment, his lips hovering, giving me a chance to tell him no. When I don't, he kisses me. His lips are soft and commanding, moving with mine as one hand moves up to cup my jaw.

When he pulls back, I am breathless. My head is running a million miles a minute as heat rushes to my face.

I wrap my hands into his hair and pull him back to me, pressing my chest against his as I hungrily take every kiss he has to give me. When we are both gasping for breath, I pull back and rest my head on his chest. His arms circle around me and hold me close, but only for a moment before a single finger is snaking under my chin and bringing my gaze up to his.

His eyes stare into mine, unmoving and unblinking. If I wanted to look away, I wouldn't be able to. His finger is like an iron grip on my chin.

"You are beautiful, Stella. You do not need me to tell you that, but I will every second until every word that idiot ever said is washed from your head. Do you hear me?"

I nod, weakly. His thumb brushes gently over my lips.

"I want you to think of my lips on yours now, not his. He never touched you. He is nothing."

His words whisper over my skin.

"Oliver, I-"

I am not sure what I was about to say and it doesn't matter, because my phone ringing in my pocket startles us both. We jump apart as if we have just committed the biggest sin. It's one in the morning. Who could possibly be calling me right now?

"Sorry," I mutter, pulling my phone from my pocket and looking down at the screen.

Beth's smiling face beams up at me. Part of me wants to ignore it and pretend my perfect little bubble hasn't just been popped. The larger part of me, the part that always wins, knows that if Beth is calling me this late, I have to answer. She wouldn't call me if it wasn't an emergency. Another voice whispers in my ear, 'because she knows you won't answer', but I ignore it.

"Beth?" I ask, bringing the phone up to my ear.

Oliver is watching me, his eyebrows knit together. The surprise of the call forced us apart about a foot and the distance feels like miles in the chill. I'm not cold, but I use one hand to pull the blanket tighter around me.

At first, there is no sound on the other end.

"Beth?" I ask again.

This time, there is a muffled sob. I straighten, every nerve in my body suddenly on alert.

"Beth, what's wrong?"

Oliver's back straightens too. His jaw tightens as he reads my features.

There is another muffled cry and a sniffle.

"Stella, I know we haven't been talking, and I know you hate me…" she trails off.

"I don't hate you."

"I…I'm pregnant, Stella." She finally manages between whimpers. "It's not Luke's. I don't know what to do. What am I supposed to do?"

"Take a deep breath, Beth."

"You don't understand! He hits me, Stella. He hits me and he yells at me, and I couldn't take it anymore. I've been seeing this other guy and he's kind to me, and he treats me right, and…and I didn't plan on getting pregnant."

I can't speak. I can barely breathe.

"Beth-"

"I know I have to tell Luke. I know I have to call off the wedding. I know. But I can't. Stella, I'm scared."

My hand is gripping the phone so tightly, I'm worried I am going to have imprints from it on my palm. Either that, or it is going to slip from my grasp due to the cold sweat I have broken into.

I must look as panicked as I feel, because Oliver looks extremely worried.

"Beth, have you gone to the cops?" I ask once I've finally found my words.

"Of course I have, but he's Luke. He's shiny smile, always says the right thing, father's head of the select board, Luke. No one believes me." She's getting hysterical, her screams echoing out of the phone.

I barely think before the next words leave my mouth. Buried within me is a girl who always knew what to do, who would have handled this situation months ago if she'd just picked up the damn phone. I call on her for a moment, forgetting every stupid reason I ignored every call and reminding myself that girl still exists.

"Beth, listen to me. This is what you are going to do. You are going to go to Daven's house right now. I will call him and let him know you are coming. You are going to sleep there and in the morning, you are going to drive to Bar Harbor. You are not going to tell Luke where you are going. We are going to figure this out together, okay?"

For a moment, I think she's hung up.

Then her shaky yes comes and I exhale.

Chapter Ten

Aunt Milly is pacing the kitchen. I called out of work as soon as the diner opened this morning and woke Aunt Milly up minutes later. I have no idea what time Beth will be here. I've just gotten done filling Aunt Milly in on our phone call last night and she is considering every angle in the way she always does.

"That poor girl," She finally says. "You can't blame yourself, Stella. You had no idea."

I know she means well, but it's hard not to blame myself. Beth has been calling me for weeks and I have just ignored her for my own selfish reasons.

And what's worse, part of me was angry with her when she called last night. She interrupted a moment between Oliver and I, and part of me wanted to be mad at her for it.

"Luke always seemed like such a nice boy." She sighs. Something inside of me screams, because that's just the point, isn't it? It's always the nice boys who get away with it, because no one believes it to be true.

"You can go to work," I tell her, plopping a pop tart into the toaster and pressing it down. "I'll be okay waiting for her."

"Are you sure?"

I nod.

Across the street, out the kitchen's big glass windows, I can see Oliver's house. He's not home. He would have left for work two hours ago.

Caleb is however. He's sitting in the sloping sand beside the house, looking down at his phone. Maybe I will go hang out with him to pass the time. Nat's at work today, where I should be. Leah, the young girl who answered when I called out, assured me it was fine and nobody was mad. But all I can keep thinking about is the breakfast rush and how I've screwed my friends over.

No matter what I do, someone always loses.

"Go ahead," I turn around to give Aunt Milly a quick hug and peck on the cheek.

"Call me if you need anything." She says as she hurries out the door, already late.

I eat my poptart and drink a mug of coffee in silence, as my mind screams at me. My brain is on fire. My two worlds are colliding and I have no idea how to grasp either of them.

Finishing my coffee, I rinse out the mug and jog upstairs. I need to have at least some of these thoughts somewhere that isn't clogging up my head.

Grabbing the journal from the attic, I sit on the front porch and open to the next clean page.

He makes me see things in myself I thought were long gone. When I am with him, I'm not sure I'm really as broken as I think I am. Maybe I am crazy. I probably am. This will all be over by the end of the summer anyway. But for right now, is it

so wrong to want to hold on to this tiny piece of feeling okay?
When I'm with him, I don't feel like such a fuck up.

I scribble the words down, hoping getting them out of my head will make the rest of the day easier.

I glance back to page one.

1. *Wear more skirts. I like skirts.*
2. *Stop being so afraid of everything.*
3. *Stop falling for Oliver. You Idiot.*
4. *Stop being suck a shitty fucking friend.*
5. *Stop thinking about Leo. It's in the past.*
6. *Figure out how not to push everyone away (good luck)*

I am already failing terribly at the entire list, but just for fun, I scribble in one more. What could it hurt?

7. *Look at yourself the way Oliver looks at you.*

I bring the journal back upstairs and tuck it into my bedside stand. With the entire day ahead of me and no idea what time Beth will be here, I suddenly feel very lost.

I change into a pair of shorts and a t-shirt, brushing through my hair and grabbing my phone from its charger.

Caleb is still scrolling through his phone when my feet hit the sand on the other side of the road. His signature cap is resting on his knee, his free hand occasionally spinning it around or giving it a flick.

A woman pushing a baby stroller gives me a dirty look as I wait for her to pass. I ignore it. The world seems so angry lately.

"Hey," I say, settling down into the sand beside Caleb. He glances up, a wide smile on his face. For a moment I wonder about his brother, Chris. Did he look like Caleb? How is it possible that Caleb is always so happy when something so terrible happened to his family? Maybe I'm not the only one good at faking it.

"Hey. Want to help me order Nat a dress?"

"She has you ordering her a dress?" I laugh.

"She has me do a lot of things." He mumbles.

"What do you mean?"

He runs a hand through his bright red hair and his phone falls into the sand. I pick it up and begin scrolling through the site he is on. All of the dresses are beautiful. I click on a white one with light blue flowers covering the entire thing that looks lightweight and feminine. I put it in his cart and sit the phone back down between us.

A tired smile rests on his lips, but it doesn't reach his eyes.

"I'm in love with her," he finally mumbles. "I'm in love with her, but she's getting married."

I was not expecting that.

"Did you guys ever date?"

"No," he sighs. "We've always been super close. But she was always not ready when I was and I wasn't when she was. We're like the titanic."

"The titanic?"

"Yeah, you know. Like always missing each other."

"You mean like ships passing in the night? That's the saying. The titanic definitely hit something," I nudge him gently. He laughs, but again, the sound is weak.

"Yeah, I guess," he shrugs. "So, I pick out dresses and I hold her hand when she cries and I agree to be her maid of honor-"

"Her maid of honor?"

He laughs.

"Yeah. She doesn't have many girl friends."

"Caleb," I lean against him. "I am sorry."

"Don't be," he shrugs. "Small problem."

"You sound like me," I say.

"How so?"

"Everyone's problems are always bigger than mine. One thing I learned in therapy and never actually listened to but maybe you will. Your problems are still valid, no matter how small they may seem."

Caleb glances over at me. He has settled his hat back on his head. I'm not sure why, but he doesn't look entirely complete without it.

"Hey Stella, you want to do something fun with me?"

"Sure," I shrug. "I gotta stay close though."

"Okay." He jumps up and grabs my hand, yanking me to my feet with him.

Before I know it, we are hopping over to the closest tourist bike rental and renting bikes. They are crazy expensive and I am sure I have seen bikes outfront of his house, but he claims it is all part of the Maine experience.

The bikes are rusty and they squeak terribly as we make our way down the pavement. We have to dodge between people who give us side stares and glare at us. On the road we almost get hit several times by people not paying attention as they take in the sites or spending too much time watching their GPS rather than watching the road.

But Caleb is laughing and I like to hear him laugh.

He stops outfront of a brick building close to the end of town. The windows have white curtains covering them. The front door has stone steps leading up to it. It doesn't look incredibly inviting. The words Bar Harbor Hope are displayed over the door.

"What's this?" I ask, propping my bike beside his next to the door.

"This is where Oliver works. It should be his lunch break any minute now." Suddenly my heart is in my throat at the thought of seeing him again today. It doesn't feel as if I saw him only a few hours ago.

He jogs up the front steps and holds the door open for me. I pause for a minute, not sure if I should follow. The old me would turn and run but I'm trying to be better. So I take a breath and follow Caleb up the stairs. The crisis center opens up into a cramped entryway with only two chairs and a front desk. Behind the front desk is an older looking woman with graying brown hair and a fuzzy purple cardigan.

Her smile beams at us as soon as we walk in.

"Hey, Caleb! Here to see Olly?"

"Yes ma'am." Caleb leans on the desk. "Have you met my friend here? Stella." He leans in closer to her as she smiles and whispers. "Olly has the hots for her."

She laughs and I flush red.

"Caleb," I try to shush him, but Caleb isn't the kind of guy who can be shushed. He just winks at me and I feel my face getting hotter. I should have listened to my gut and stayed outside.

"Nice to meet you, hon," she smiles at me. "You must be Mildred's niece. She doesn't stop talking about you. That woman loves you."

"You know Aunt Milly?"

"Everyone knows your Aunt Milly. After your Grandma passed, she really came in here and helped patch stuff up. She's been a staple to this community since the moment she parked her car outfront of that old house," the woman laughs. "I'm Burny. Let her know you saw me and tell her I said hi."

"Will do," I say, confusion lacing my thoughts.

My Aunt is a lovable person, but I had no idea what she meant to this town. When she'd moved, for the longest time I held a resentment towards her for only visiting every once in a while when the drive was only five hours. I guess a part of me still holds that feeling towards her. I feel guilty hearing the other side of the story.

"I'll see if Oliver is available," Burny smiles and walks away through a door behind the desk.

Caleb spins around and gives me a wide smile.

"We could both use some Olly time."

"Olly time?"

"Olly has a way of making people feel better," he says, wrapping an arm around my shoulder. "Just by existing."

"I thought that was just a feeling I got," I admit, leaning into the feeling. Caleb feels safe, secure.

"Oh believe me," Caleb shakes his head and his red hair hits me in the cheek. "He has done some serious work on himself. Makes people see him differently."

"Differently?"

"He wasn't always this way. He's come a long way."

I want to ask him so many questions. What he means. Who he used to be. Of course, I know some things. I know about the drugs and vandalism, I know he struggled with mental health. I know these things, but I am hungry for information. I am greedy for it. I want to know every little thing there is to know about Oliver, and I want to know it now.

I know it isn't right to ask his friend these things though, so I press my lips together.

I don't have to keep them closed for long, because soon Oliver is coming through the door, following Burny.

He looks tired. He has an energy drink in one hand and a half eaten grinder in the other.

"Dude, you got lunch without me?" Caleb sounds offended, placing a hand over his heart.

"Phones exist for a reason, man." Oliver laughs. His expression changes when his gaze goes from Caleb to me. I try to keep my heart from beating too quickly when I realize the look he gives me has a wider smile; one that touches his eyes.

"I have a few minutes," he adds once his eyes fall on me.

I feel a smile spreading over my face almost as fast as the burning heat spreading over my cheeks.

We take his lunch on the front steps. He grabs a bag of chips and an ice coffee from the back, and the three of us share the chips while he finishes the rest.

"I get off work in half an hour," he tells us.

"Short day?" Caleb asks.

"Not many beds are full today. I decided to take the second half as personal time."

I swallow down the salty chip before fully swallowing it. Caleb just shrugs, completely unaware of the reason, but I know.

"You didn't have to do that." I say.

"I know."

Caleb is still staring off down the road at a group of people daring to weave out into traffic. He's elbowing me and pointing, trying to get us both to give it our full attention.

My eyes however are glued to Oliver and he hasn't blinked or looked away from me.

Everything I thought I knew about meeting people, about making friendships, about falling in love; all of it was a lie. I know for certain at this moment, if love is not what I feel for Oliver, it is something dangerously close.

And that scares the shit out of me.

Chapter Eleven

Beth is standing on Aunt Milly's front porch when I get home. And she isn't alone.

At first, I think my eyes are playing tricks on me.

I blink once and then I blink again.

Caleb and I returned our bike rentals and then Oliver picked us up in his truck. He's just parked out front of his house and I'm standing on the side of the road, staring at Beth and Leo like they are figments of my imagination. My stomach leaps into my throat and I feel like I am going to be sick.

There is no way that Leo is standing beside her. *Pig. Disgusting. Ugly.* Shut up.

"What's wrong?" Oliver tugs on my arm gently.

I shake my head and suck in a deep breath, feeling like I was suffocating and he reminded me how to breathe.

"Nothing," I lie. "Thank you for taking the afternoon off for me. I'll call you."

I don't turn and look at him as I barely glance across the road and cross it.

"Hey, Stella." Beth's voice is weak. She looks exhausted and frail. Her back is hunched over. Her hair is the same black it's always been, but it's frizzy and unkept, tossed into a bun on top of her head.

For a moment, I can't even think about the fact that Leo is standing beside her.

For a moment, that doesn't matter.

For a moment, it doesn't matter that we haven't talked in months. It doesn't matter that our friendship hasn't been the same in years. None of it matters because that is my friend, and she is so clearly broken.

I pull her into a hug and hold her against my chest. She shrinks, her body all but folding into mine. I want to cry at how small she feels against my chest.

When she finally pulls back, there are tears running down her face.

"I had no idea what to do." She says.

"You are safe now," I tell her, holding her shoulders and staring into her deep brown eyes. "We will figure it out."

"Thank you for this, Stella," Leo speaks up.

I am forced to look over at him.

He doesn't look like he's changed at all. Old memories are dragged up as I look into his amber eyes. His golden hair is cut a tad shorter than it used to be. He's still just as tall, just as fit. The biggest difference is the jeans and t-shirt rather than the polo and khakis he used to wear every day in school.

My mouth is dry and I can't find words.

"I know I should have told you," Beth pulls my attention back to her. "We've only been seeing each other for a few months…"

"It's okay," I force a smile onto my lips. "Come on. I'll show you around."

It's odd, having Beth back in my life.

It feels forced. It feels wrong but it also feels right. At the same time, Leo is this extension that won't go away. Just his presence reminds me of everything I've done wrong; including turning away my best friend when she needed me just because I was ashamed of who I am. Ashamed because he made me feel less than human.

"Maine looks good on you," Beth sniffles as the three of us sit around the kitchen table. I've poured us all lemonade in Aunt Milly's crystal glasses. I feel as if I'm pretending to be older and wiser than I am.

"Thanks," I take a sip from my glass. What do I say in response? She looks worn down and frazzled. Do I tell her she looks tired? I settle with a kinder fact instead. "It's been so long since I've seen you."

I don't feel my eyes slide sideways at Leo but they must, because Beth is quickly shaking her head.

"This just happened, Stella," she waves a hand between the two of them. "I never planned on being pregnant with Leo's baby, hell I didn't plan on being pregnant for a very long time. Life has been anything but predictable lately."

Before I can get a word in, Leo is clearing his throat. He's been mostly silent since they showed up. A very large part of me wishes he'd stay that way.

"Please don't blame Beth," he says, displaying an air of confidence that immediately gets under my skin. "Everything I've done is my fault."

Beth sucks in a shaky breath, casting a look sideways at Leo and then back at me. She was never one that let someone else speak for her, but that appears to be exactly what she's doing.

I simply shrug, shoving every bottled emotion towards either of them I have so far down it's as if it never even existed. Healthy, right?

"Don't worry about it," and then because Beth looks like she's about to cry, I look directly at her and add, "I'm here for you, Beth. I'm not mad."

The air fills with tension and no one speaks as time ticks slowly by on the clock.

I'm the first to break the silence.

We sip lemonade and talk about work and weather and superficial things, all of us avoiding direct eye contact for what feels like an eternity.

Aunt Milly gets home and I finally breathe.

She makes dinner and I make small talk.

"I am going to go stay with Nat tonight," I say once we are finished eating and the table is clean.

Beth's brows scrunch together. Leo is busy scrolling through his phone. Aunt Milly hasn't stopped fussing over Beth and barely looks up when I speak. I appreciate how easily she's taken her in.

"You don't have to do that. We can sleep in the living room."

"No, you won't," I tell her. "Take my room. It's fine. I already let Nat know I was coming."

I don't have the energy for the truth tonight. Judging by the quick look Aunt Milly does give me, she doesn't believe me anyway.

I run upstairs and grab some things from the attic. A change of clothing, my toothbrush, my journal.

Once outside, it's not my car I run to.

I'm already across the street and knocking on the door when my mind catches up with my body.

Oliver answers on the second knock.

"Stella-" I'm not sure what expression is on my face, but whatever it is causes him to fall silent.

"Can I stay here tonight?"

He nods and moves aside.

*   *   *

"Back up," Oliver is pacing the room. I am sitting in the center of his bed and my head feels like it is going to explode. I don't want to talk about Beth or Leo anymore. I don't want to, but I know he deserves an explanation. "The father of her baby is Leo? *The* Leo? And he's here?"

I nod.

"He's here." I repeat. "I think he's the dad."

"Are you okay?"

"As okay as I'm going to be," I sigh, because I know lying is a moot point with him. "I don't want to talk about it anymore. I don't want to think about him anymore."

His sigh is low and guttural as he runs a hand through his hair.

"Kiss me." I say, pulling every bit of confidence I can from deep in my chest.

His eyes scan up my body slowly and when they finally land on my face, his lips part slightly.

"If you want it," he says, his voice low. "You are going to have to come and get it."

I stand on shaky feet and close the distance between us, welcoming the distraction. He is standing in the center of the room in gym shorts and a t-shirt. I press my palms to his chest and shudder. He is so perfect. He smells like pine and soap.

He tilts his head down slightly, his lips an inch from mine. Letting my hands slide up his chest to his shoulders, I feel his sliding around my waist, pulling me against him. I melt into the touch as I close the space between us and press my lips to his.

It's better than the first time.

This time starts slow and sweet. It isn't rushed like it was on the beach. It doesn't feel like we are racing to beat time. I savor every moment as I taste his lips on mine and only pull back when it is getting hard to breathe.

"I love kissing you," he murmurs against my cheek, his breath wafting over my skin.

"Make me forget every reason I feel so utterly broken," I whisper. His kisses stop, his lips resting against my neck for a moment.

"Being broken is beautiful," he finally whispers.

"Show me."

"Are you sure?"

I nod, feeling his lips move over my skin softly as I do. Returning his attention back to kissing me, his hands softly grasp the skin just under my shirt on my hips as he walks me backwards.

My back presses against the wall and I moan at the feeling of his warm hand dusting softly over my belly.

"If you want to stop, just tell me to stop," he whispers. How can clearly spoken consent sound so utterly sexy?

"Please don't stop."

He chuckles, the sound vibrating against my lips. His hair brushes over my shoulders and it tickles, sending a shiver down my spine. His hands on my sides are sending a wonderful tingle directly between my legs.

I shift and he laughs again, this time softer.

"What do you want, Stella?"

I take a deep, shaky breath.

"I'm not good at this," I admit, the nerves beginning to set in. Voices in my head convincing me I am not good enough to be with a man like Oliver.

"You are perfect, baby."

Baby. He called me baby.

"I'm a virgin," I admit, squeezing my eyes shut, expecting him to pull away. To my surprise, the kisses he is pecking across my collarbone, up my neck, and across my face continue.

"Thank you for telling me," he breathes between kissing my nose and kissing the corner of my mouth. "We don't have to do anything you don't want to do."

I gulp. Fuck that's sexy.

Using one shaky hand, I press a finger to his jaw and guide his lips back to mine. He moves easily under my touch, kissing me with so much passion I feel my knees buckling. I thought that was only in the movies.

His hands scoop under my ass and pull my legs around him, pressing me against the wall as he holds me to him.

"Oliver," I sigh into his kiss.

"Tell me what you need, baby."

"You." I moan.

In one swift motion, he's taken me from the wall to the bed. He lays me back gently into the comforter and hovers over me, being careful to keep his weight off of me as he kisses a trail from my face to the v in my shirt and back up.

"I have been imagining this moment since the first time I saw you on the beach," he murmurs, pulling back so I can see his eyes.

So green. So beautiful. And full of lust. Lust for me. I can't breathe in the best way possible.

I need his shirt off.

I yank with fumbling hands on the hem. Understanding my desire, he kneels between my legs, pulling his shirt off himself. God, he's gorgeous. He has more abs than I wish to count, his tan skin warm and soft under my touch. And the tattoos. God, they are everywhere.

I trace a single finger over his torso as he smiles down at me.

"You are beautiful." I murmur.

"Your turn," he gently grabs the hem of my shirt and waits for me to nod before lifting it up and over my head. I half sit up to make it easier and then fall back into the pillows, braless beneath him.

His eyes stare for a moment and I feel myself turning bright red.

"That blush," he whispers, kissing my cheek. "Is agonizingly beautiful."

My whole body quivers as his thumb circles over my already peaked nipple. At my reaction, his smile widens and he does it again.

I feel my back arching off the bed as he continues to work my nipple. He then palms both of my breasts, his large, warm hands fitting perfectly over me.

He leans down and kisses me and I feel as if I might explode.

As he continues to kiss me, his hands exploring my upper half, I feel the thoughts nudging into my brain. Nerves, anxiety, and questions circle my thoughts like a lion circling its prey. They are not welcome, but I know I can't ignore them.

Oliver doesn't deserve the questions currently residing in my head. Once I give him all of me, what is keeping him from leaving? Once he sees who I am, truly, what is stopping this from being over?

Oliver hasn't given me a single reason to think he'd ever leave. He kisses me as if his life depends on it and looks at me as if I am his source of air.

Yet I still can't stop the thoughts of self doubt and self hatred from eating into the moment.

My breath is quickening and not from lust.

I press a hand to his chest and shove just a bit. He pulls back immediately, his eyes searching mine.

I bite my lip, afraid to say it.

"Baby, it's okay. Tell me."

"I don't…" I trail off. "I don't think I can have sex tonight. I don't…I don't think I'm ready."

He nuzzles his face into the crook of my neck and gently bites down on my skin. I whimper, my head tossing back at the feeling of bliss that one motion sends through my entire body.

"We go at your pace," he whispers. One hand trails down my body and tugs at the waistband of my bottoms. A single finger dips below the line, brushing gently across the thin fabric of my panties. I suck in a sharp breath, rotating my hips upward, aching for his touch to go lower.

"I want to make you feel good," he whispers against my skin. I whimper as his finger dips lower. "Tell me to stop, Stella."

"I don't want you to stop," I moan.

His hand disappears below my panties, his finger easily finding my clit. He rubs his thumb gently over the bundle of nerves, all while paying close attention to my raised nipples.

My back arches off the bed as he works his finger over and around my clit, his expert tongue taking a nipple into his mouth and gently sucking.

"Do you feel broken now?" He growls against my skin, the vibrations almost sending me over the edge.

"I feel…" my breath catches in my throat as he sucks at my nipple again. I am going to explode. "I feel everything."

"That's right baby. Let go for me."

I do, as if hearing Oliver say I am not so worthless is all I needed to allow myself to break. I let go with a loud moan, feeling it in every nerve ending in my body. My fingertips and toes even tingle.

The moment the feeling fades, tears are rushing down my cheeks and I am sobbing uncontrollably. Oliver removes his hand from my pants and pulls me to his chest, settling us against his pillow and running a hand softly over my hair.

"I'm sorry, do you want me to…" I suck in a shaky breath through my sobs. "I shouldn't be crying, that's such a mood killer. You didn't even get to come."

He chuckles lightly, but not in a way to embarrass me. With a single finger he lifts my chin up to look at him and brushes a kiss over my trembling lips.

"I wanted to make you feel good, Stella. I am a patient man. Don't you worry about me. Are you okay?"

Am I okay?

I assess myself for a quick moment. Physically, I am more than okay. Physically, I am better than I have been in a long time. Emotionally, I feel as if I just got off a rollercoaster and my head is spinning out of control.

Are orgasms always like this or just ones somehow tied to your self worth?

"That was intense." I finally answer.

"I know you think you aren't enough, Stella," Oliver muses. My head is against his chest again and I can't see his eyes. I almost want to take a peak, but knowing how intense they always are, I would probably start sobbing again. As my breathing is just starting to calm down, I keep my head pressed firmly against his chest, feeling the rise and fall and the steady beat of his heart. "I know you think you aren't worthy of love. I am going to spend this summer worshiping you until you believe that you are more than enough and always have been."

I don't answer. Words are caught in my throat and any I can think of saying don't feel as if they would be nearly enough. Instead I nuzzle my face closer to his chest and close my eyes, allowing myself for the second time tonight to truly feel. I had forgotten how good it could be to focus on yourself for just a moment.

The tears begin again and Oliver pulls me closer.

I am a complete mess and for some reason I can't quite understand why but, he doesn't seem at all to mind.

*   *   *

I wake up topless with my head on Oliver's chest, and immediately, I feel guilty.

What right do I have to this moment when Beth is over at Aunt Milly's having one of the worst times of her life? I am selfish. I can feel the self hatred radiating down to my toes.

Quietly, I stand from the bed.

It shifts slightly, but Oliver doesn't wake up. He is incredible, even when he is sleeping. His chest rises and falls softly as he pulls the blanket further up his chest in his sleep. I want so badly to crawl back into bed and curl back next to him, never leaving.

Instead, I pull my baggy t-shirt back on and leave the room as quietly as I can.

Thankfully, Caleb isn't up either.

The town is barely awake this early in the morning, so crossing the road and tiptoeing inside is easy. The door squeaks as I shut it softly behind me and turn around.

Beth is sitting at the kitchen table with a cup of coffee in her hands. All of the lights are out and the room is dark, lit only by the rising sun that has barely broken over the horizon. She's already dressed, her hair already in braids over her shoulders. She's been crying.

I pad over to her and sit in the chair beside her.

"Listen, Beth," I begin, but she shakes her head and raises a hand to stop me.

Biting down on my lip, I prepare myself for whatever she is about to say. Whatever it is, I deserve it. I've been a terrible friend.

"How did we get here?" She finally whispers. Her voice is raspy from unshed tears. My heart aches at the sound of it.

"I don't know."

"We were both going places, weren't we?" She rubs her eyes with both hands. "It feels like only yesterday we were graduating High School. We were so full of hope. What the hell happened?"

"Beth, we're only twenty two," I say, even though the words fall flat to my own ears. I know that means nothing. I know we both feel like the world is ending and we aren't quick enough to save it. I know that. But that isn't what she needs to hear right now. So I channel my inner Oliver and push whatever words I think I -I mean Beth- might need to hear out of my mouth. "There is still so much time."

"I let a man abuse me, Stella. I let him walk all over me. I stopped going to classes, stopped doing my homework. I'm failing. And why? All for some man who tells me he loves me? And if that weren't bad enough," her laugh is high pitched and hysterical. "Well now I'm pregnant and it's not even his baby. Because not only am I a disappointment, I'm also a whore."

I want to fix it.

I want to say every perfect thing that I know she needs to hear.

My tongue is like sandpaper in my mouth. Am I even the person she needs right now? I know what she needs. I know how to be the friend she remembers I once was. I'm just not entirely sure that's me anymore. How long do I pretend for her sake to still be the put together girl who always knew how to fix everything?

Maybe I should at least hug her. She is falling apart and maybe I could be the glue.

Instead, I just stare at her.

"Oh honey," Aunt Milly's voice startles us both. She sweeps into the kitchen, her nightgown looking to me like a cape as she winds her arms around Beth and pulls her to her chest.

Beth begins crying again, her tears soaking Aunt Milly's nightgown immediately. She soothes her hands over her hair and makes shushing noises, reminding me of when I was a small girl and every little problem was life altering. Only this is a big problem. And it is life altering. How did we get here? Such a good question.

"Life can seem so impossible sometimes, can't it sweetie?" Aunt Milly pulls back, her hands on either side of Beth's face.

I can't sit here any longer.

I feel helpless, responsible, and sick.

The clock is my friend this morning. I need to be at work in twenty minutes.

Standing silently, I go to Aunt Milly's room instead of my own where I know Leo must still be. I am much shorter than her and a bit rounder, but a pair of black cloth shorts fit me okay. I keep the same white t-shirt on from last night and just borrow a sports bra that is tight, but will do the job. Anything to avoid the attic right now.

I slip out the side door.

My gut is twisted with guilt, but I can't be the person that comforts Beth right now. She has Aunt Milly. That will always be better than me.

No one comes out of the house as I start my car and drive off. No one even looks out the window. I wonder if they even realize I am gone.

My phone dings as I pull down the road, stopping at a stop sign to let a group walk across the street. I glance down and read the text.

Oliver: I missed you when I woke up.

Feeling the sting of tears in the corner of my eye from guilt pushing me over the edge, I blink and take a deep breath. Before moving the car again, I quickly text back.

Stella: Sorry. Have to work.

Expecting another text from him, I quickly put my phone on silent and toss it into the bottom of my bag. I can't deal with more feelings of not being enough right now. I don't need Oliver to hate me too.

Nat is a bundle of nerves as soon as I walk in the door, her energy running higher than normal. Which means she is basically a human pinball, bouncing around the diner without catching her breath.

"Carrie will be here tomorrow!" She shrieks. "Which of course means the dress Caleb bought for me for the day she gets here won't be here in time, so I need you to help me pick a different outfit."

She pulls out her phone and swipes through choices as I tie on my apron.

My head feels heavy. I blink several times, forcing myself to stare at the screen and actually comprehend what I am looking at.

"I like that one." I tell her, nodding my chin towards the second. She's taken a photo in a full length mirror of her with bedhead wearing a pink ruffled top and a white skirt. It's cute. If I'm being honest, I didn't even really see the others though.

"Are you okay?" She asks.

No, I want to scream.

Everything is messed up. The only place I want to be right now is with Oliver, but instead I am here. The only person I want to be talking to is Oliver, but instead I am here. And the worst part is, there isn't a universe in which I actually deserve to be with him.

He is good. He is light. He cares about other people. He puts others' needs before his.

My best friend needs me and all I can think of is being anywhere but where she is.

People like me don't belong with people like Oliver. Not in this universe, and not in any other.

"Yeah," I shrug, plastering the fakest smile onto my lips. "I'm fine."

She doesn't believe me. It doesn't matter.

I walk away, blinking back tears.

Chapter Twelve

"There is a super hot guy asking for you outfront," Nat wiggles her eyebrows at me.

This stupid shift is almost over. I have grown to love Nat's company, but today, her energy is irritating me. I want to crawl under the covers and go to sleep and never wake up. I want to be in any body but my own.

"Oh yeah?" I ask.

"It's Olly." She laughs. "Go ahead, leave a little early. We're slow anyway."

You don't have to ask me twice.

"I'll see you tomorrow, okay?"

She nods.

"You better not forget."

How would I? She's only been talking about Carrie coming home nonstop all shift. They are having a party at her apartment to welcome her back. I promised I would be there days ago, and now I am wishing I could take it back.

Doing that would only add to the list of reasons I am a terrible person. That is not a list that needs to be added to.

I clock out, untie my apron, and grab my things from the back. Leaving, I make sure to avoid eye contact with everyone. I don't want to explain myself.

I trudge outfront. I can't help the light that fills my chest as soon as I see Oliver waiting for me. He's leaning against the counter, a smirk set on the edge of his lips. He doesn't work today or tomorrow. I remember that being said at one point last night between kissing and cuddling.

"Hey," I smile tiredly.

"Come on. I want to take you somewhere."

I don't object. I am too tired to object.

We take his truck and ride in complete silence. He doesn't try to start a conversation and neither do I. I appreciate it; the silence. I enjoy not having to fill every moment with noise.

We drive well out of town. Along the coast; we are following the ocean. I watch out the window as the waves lap up on cliff edges and against beaches. We have been driving for over half an hour when he finally pulls off onto a side road that ends in a hidden beach. It's empty and shrouded in trees.

It feels like it's going to rain tonight. It will be the first time since I came to the island that we've had less than perfect weather. I am almost excited for it.

It's a little after one, but there is a chill coming in off the ocean.

Oliver grabs a blanket from the back seat and wraps an arm around me as we walk down to the water and sit just in front of it.

I nuzzle into his chest, allowing him to wrap the blanket around both of us. Closing my eyes, I take deep breaths and focus on our bodies, trying to block out every unwelcome thought.

"I should be at Aunt Milly's," I finally admit outloud. As hard as I am trying to keep the thought out, it is the only one that really matters, because it is the truth. I should be there for her.

"Is Beth alone?"

"No. Leo is there, and Aunt Milly too I think. But I should be. I am her friend. Or at least I used to be."

The silence stretches on for a long moment before he clears his throat, the motion vibrating my ear against his chest. I nestle closer. I can't get close enough.

"Do you need me to agree with you or give you advice?" He asks.

My eyebrows knit together and I pull back to look at his face. He looks down at me, no trace of humor on his features. He reaches up and brushes a strand of hair from my face as I stare at him.

"What?"

"It's something I learned in therapy," he says. "Sometimes people don't need advice or help. Sometimes they just want their feelings to be validated. I can give you either, baby, you just need to tell me which one you need."

I swallow hard and actually think about it. Which one do I need?

"I think… does it make me a bad person if I say validation?"

"No," he chuckles, dusting a kiss on the tip of my nose. His breath smells of mint, wafting over my face. "You have done what was in your means to do at the time, Stella. You gave her a safe space to get away. Nobody is perfect, but you helped her when she needed it, and that counts. Don't you think so?"

I know I need to be honest with Oliver. For two reasons. One, I am not sure I am actually capable of lying to him. And two, even if I were, he would see right through my bullshit in a heartbeat.

"I don't even want to think about her, Oliver. Every time I do, I feel guilty. I ignored her calls for weeks. And the first night she is here, I makeout with you. Maybe not everyone is perfect, but they aren't all assholes either."

To my surprise, Oliver doesn't laugh.

"I know how you feel. When Chris killed himself, I didn't even go to the funeral. I felt so guilty for months afterward, even talking to Caleb about him made me sick. You aren't an asshole for avoiding your problems, Stella. You're human."

I laugh, a cold, humorless laugh.

"Ten things to do before I go. Add, stop being so fucking human."

He chuckles, and then a hand slides under my chin and raises my face to meet his. He holds me steady, gripping my jaw so that if I wanted to look away, I couldn't. His hands are commanding, but gentle. A thumb rubs over my chin as he tilts his head to the side, contemplating me.

"If you weren't so fucking human," he says, his voice low and smooth, "then maybe this wouldn't feel so good."

He lowers his lips to mine and kisses me, a soft, gentle kiss. There is no urgency, little passion. It's almost a peck, but butterflies soar straight to my belly. He kisses me again, this time longer, his teeth grazing my bottom lip. I curl closer to him, letting my arms slide out of the blanket to wrap around his neck.

"See, this is the problem," I groan against his lips. "I shouldn't be doing this right now."

"Do you want to stop?"

I shake my head, feeling the guilt gnaw at me as I do.

"No. But I should."

He pulls back, placing a hand on either side of my face. Staring into his eyes, a feeling of safety washes through my body that is so foreign, I almost turn away from it. Instead, I embrace it, welcoming it into my veins. It feels warm and soft, like a familiar hug.

"We can go. If you want to go back to your Aunt's, I will take you there right now. But don't do it because you feel obligated Stella. Do it because you want to."

I swallow hard.

"I don't want to. I want to keep kissing you."

His hands slide up into my hair and he is kissing me again, this time with more passion than I can handle. His tongue gently coaxes open my lips and flits inside, twirling with my own. I moan into his mouth and feel the edges of his turn up into a smile.

"I love the sounds you make, baby," one hand slides down and palms my breast over the thin material of my t-shirt and sports bra. My next moan is silenced by his lips on mine.

My back arches into his touch.

I uncurl myself from his arms and from the blanket and wrap my legs around him, straddling him in the sand. Wrapping his arms around my waist, he pulls me closer. I can feel all of him pressed against me. The feeling is sinful. I never want it to stop.

"I want to taste you." He moans against my neck.

"Huh?" I am breathless, gasping and red.

"I want to be between your legs Stella. I want to know what you taste like."

Yep. Definitely bright red.

"Here?" My voice is a squeak.

"Only if you are comfortable. I promise it is safe. Barely anyone knows about this place." How does he manage to make even that sound sexy?

"Okay," I agree.

He grinds me closer to him, his hardened length pressing against my stomach.

"Oliver," I moan.

"Do you trust me?"

I nod quickly.

"More than anyone," I add, because he is so open and honest with me. Doesn't he deserve the same from me, even if it tears me apart to even try?

"Good." He says, pulling away. His eyes are gleaming. Pulling away, he unwraps the blanket from our legs and lays it on the sand. Rolling me over onto the soft blanket, he settles between my legs and hooks his thumbs into the waistband of my shorts.

I am squirming underneath him, the feeling between my legs no longer just an ache. His words are doing things to me I can barely stand. I need to feel him. I need him to touch me.

"Are you sure?" He asks one last time. I nod but he shakes his head. "I need words baby."

Damn, that's sexy.

"Yes, Oliver. I am sure."

His grin is the devil itself.

He hooks his thumbs in and tugs my pants and panties down at the same time, pulling them from my legs in one swift motion.

Being looked at by a man like Oliver is something I could only have dreamed of. But here he is, staring at me as if I am the most beautiful woman on the planet.

His hands are warm, grabbing my knees and easing them apart to open me to him.

"Has anyone ever gone down on you before?" He asks, his voice quiet and gentle.

I shake my head. The only boy I've ever kissed is Leo. I did give him head, not that I think I was any good. He refused to return the favor. That was as far as I had gone with anyone. Boys never found me attractive. Or I was always too awkward to know if they did. Or maybe both. It doesn't matter because Oliver isn't a boy. Oliver is a man, and he is currently looking at me like I am dessert and he is starving.

I suppress a smile.

"Tap my head or say stop if it becomes too much," He tells me. "I want to make you come so hard you see stars, baby."

God damn.

Before I can even fathom what I should say in response to that, he drops a single hand to the inside of my thigh. I shudder as the feeling of just his finger sliding across the sensitive skin there sends waves of pleasure directly to my core.

That same finger slips between my folds and his thumb gently slides over my clit. I have touched myself before, but this is a different feeling entirely.

My back arches, trying to push myself closer to his touch. He continues, gently swirling his thumb around my clit until I am moaning with pleasure. He uses his knee to gently push my legs open a bit more, and then slowly, his head dips down between my legs.

I'm not prepared for the feeling of his tongue sliding over my clit.

He starts with just a flick. Light pressure, but combined with his thumb, I gasp. He sighs and the feeling makes the ache building in my belly explode. I am not going to last much longer.

He flicks his tongue again, circling it over me as his finger slides further down. I am in heaven. I think he's said something but I'm not sure what.

"Baby."

"Yeah?" I gasp.

"Can you handle a finger?"

I nod. I have no idea if I can. My own, yes. Right now, I would let Oliver do whatever he wants to me. I am at his mercy and I don't want it any other way.

"Words." He reminds me.

"Yes, Oliver, yes."

Gently, one finger slides inside me.

As his finger works in and out of me and his tongue slides over my clit, I feel the pleasure building. I am about to tip over the edge and he knows it.

Before I know it, I am soaring. The pleasure washing through me is like no orgasm I have ever given myself before. It's somehow even better than last night. I am flying and I never want to come down. The warmth washes through my entire body in waves. I clamp my own hand over my mouth to resist the urge to scream.

When the waves have finished, Oliver sits up between my legs, grinning. He looks incredibly proud of himself. He leans down and kisses me.

"If there is anything I want you to remember that I ever say," he breathes as he leans over me, his lips inches from mine. "Is that's exactly how you deserve to be treated. Never any less than that, baby."

Chapter Thirteen

"You don't owe me any explanation, Beth," I sigh, running a hand over the rough material of my old sweats. I do not want to be sitting here on the porch with Leo and Beth sitting across from me. I wish Aunt Milly would come out from the kitchen and sit with me.

They were waiting for me when I got back with Oliver from the beach. Sitting on the porch with their legs touching. Oliver had offered to come up with me, but this is something I have to do by myself, and deep down I know it. Even if I am about to have a panic attack.

"I want to give you one," she says.

"Just let me start off by saying I am sorry," I tell her. "I am sorry for ignoring your calls. You needed me, and I wasn't there. There is no excuse I could give you that would make that okay."

She shrugs.

"We both became pretty terrible friends, Stella. That burden isn't solely on you."

I'm not going to argue that, although until this moment, I hadn't thought of it that way.

"Lucas and I haven't been right for over a year. I was faithful to him, I swear. I was. Until the anger started. At first it was just yelling. Throwing things near me but never at me," she sniffles, running a hand over her tired face. Leo grabs her other hand and holds it against his thigh. I am trying as hard as I can not to look at him at all, but he is making it difficult. I want to pretend he doesn't exist. "I couldn't take it anymore. Leo was at the bar down on Mainstreet when I went one night. I was upset, I drank a little too much, and one thing led to another. My life is falling apart, Stella. I don't know what to do."

I take a deep breath.

"We are all broken, Beth," I finally say. "What can I do to help you?"

Her brow furrows.

I can feel Oliver's voice in my head, guiding me. It is almost like I know exactly what he would say if I were the one crying right now. Maybe I should just go get Oliver. But I know the same words wouldn't mean what they do coming from his mouth as they would from mine. Not to her anyway. Right now, she needs her friend. And even if I feel as far from that girl as possible, I can pretend to be her for a moment longer.

"I think I just need to clear my head. Figure out what I am going to do."

I nod.

"This place is good for that."

"I don't want to impose," she sniffles. "I got a hotel room for two more nights up the road. I think Leo and I will go home after that. I have school and he has work… and I can't hide from Lucas forever."

"You didn't have to do that," I try to reassure her. "My room is fine."

"You've been kind enough," she says, a small smile on her lips. "Really, Stella. You didn't have to help me."

She isn't saying it, but I know she's talking about Leo. Yes, I haven't been able to get that day with him out of my head since the moment he got here. Unprocessed trauma lingering at the back of my mind just waiting for the right moment to barge to the front. But as true as that is, it was years ago. And putting that before Beth would have been wrong.

"We're still friends, Beth. Even shitty ones."

Leo hasn't said a single thing. He's silent, which is getting on my nerves as much as it makes me happy. I don't want to hear his voice, but the fact that he's not talking means he remembers that day. Does he feel bad?

It doesn't matter.

They pack their few things and leave to check into the hotel rather quickly. As honest as I was in telling her they could have stayed, I would be lying if I said I wasn't at least a tad happy to have my room back.

Although it gets rid of my excuse to go stay with Oliver again. Not that I need an excuse.

I retreat to my room and dig out my journal.

Laying in a bundle of my comforter, I prop the tattered paperback up on my knee and scribble near the bottom of the first page.

8.   Convince yourself you are not always the problem.

*   *   *

"I am freaking out Stella! Please tell me how to stop freaking out!" Nat is going to pull her hair out of her head and wear a path through her living room floor all at the same time.

I had never been to Nat's apartment before today. Today, it is dressed to the nines. Caleb, Oliver and I came over early to help her decorate it.

Now, Nat is pacing and on the verge of tears. Carrie's uber is due to arrive at any moment, and though the house is full of people waiting to greet her, Nat is acting as if we are the only ones in the room. And I am pretty sure if we don't do something quickly, she may throw up all over the couch.

"Nat." I bounce to my feet and place two hands on either side of her face. She stops her moving and stares at me, her lips pouting out and her eyes wide.

"What?"

"You love Carrie, right?"

She nods.

"And Carrie loves you."

She nods again.

"You want to marry her, right?"

She gulps and her head moves up and down one more time.

"Take a deep breath, okay? It's going to be alright."

She shakes her shoulders out and I slowly move my hands from her face. I spent most of the morning helping her with her hair. First we straightened it, and then she decided she wanted it curled instead. When we were finished with that, I used my mediocre makeup skills to help her craft brows and lengthen her eyelashes. That was all before getting into my own sundress and helping the boys decorate.

"Are you sure Beth and Leo aren't coming?" She asks, her breathing shaky. She's distracting herself with my problems and though I understand the tactic, I don't quite appreciate the turn of events that puts the attention back on me.

"They're gone." I assure her.

Aunt Milly called me this morning as I was heading into Nat's house to tell me one of her friends had seen them checking out of the hotel before sunrise.

Beth hasn't answered my calls since.

I've been trying hard not to think about it, but when Nat keeps bringing it up to change the topic from herself, it's kind of difficult.

"I think I see her Uber turning the corner!" A stout, older woman I think I've gathered is Nat's Aunt shouts from her position by the window.

"Fuck!" Nat squeaks, gripping my hand and holding on so tightly I'm afraid it's going to go numb.

Caleb and Oliver are smiling from the couch at me, but I find nothing about this funny. Okay, maybe it's a tad humorous that I have become her emotional support human for the day. But my hand would argue otherwise.

The room falls silent as we wait.

It's not a surprise party, but it might as well be.

The front door squeaks open and I barely get a look at the tall blonde who walks through, because Nat has hurled herself across the room at her.

I take the moment to stumble back towards the couch and sink between Caleb and Oliver, hoping Nat won't notice I've moved. I don't think she will, as she's currently wrapped around her fiance with her hands tangled in her hair like they are the only ones in the room.

Everyone in the room is averting their eyes, looking anywhere but at the couple of the hour.

When they finally pull apart, Nat saunters over to us with her hand in Carrie's. Carrie is beautiful. She's all legs with bright blonde hair and a glowing smile. Something about her pinched face and wandering gaze give me a lump in my throat, but I swallow over it and ignore the feeling in my stomach. My intuition hasn't always been the greatest, why would it start now?

"Guys, meet Carrie," She squeals. Carrie gives us all a small wave, partnered with the pinched smile.

"Hey."

"I need air," Caleb shoots up from his seat and brushes past Nat with his head down, all but sprinting for the door. He grabs his ball cap from a stand by the door and shoves it down backwards on his head before disappearing outside. My gaze follows him for a moment, wishing I could go with him. Somebody should check on him, make sure he's okay. Am I the only one who knows he's in love with Nat?

Oliver tugs on my arm, bringing me back to the present. With him beside me, my heart isn't kicking into overdrive. There are no lingering feelings of a panic attack on the edges of my vision. I suck in a deep breath, forcing myself to smile at Carrie. Only a second has passed, but it feels like it's been an eternity. Oliver makes everything slow down. He makes everything easier.

"Hey Carrie," He smiles. He's obviously met her before. "How was the flight?"

Nat and Carrie sit down on the coffee table in front of us and Carrie begins to tell us a story about an annoying baby on her flight that wouldn't stop crying. I try to keep myself engaged, but my brain is anywhere but here. It is with Beth, with Caleb, with Oliver and myself. I care for Nat deeply, but right now, I want to be anywhere but right here.

Selfish. Stella, you are so stupidly selfish.

Oliver squeezes my knee and I blink myself back to the present. Carrie and Nat are walking away. They don't look mad. Carrie looks like she has something important to say as she tugs Nat into a room down the hall and shuts the door behind them.

"I hope Caleb is okay," I mutter, glancing at the door. He still hasn't come back inside.

"I doubt he'll be back. He tries to be supportive of her, but it's killing him," Oliver sighs, rubbing the hand on my knee up and down in soothing strokes.

"So I'm not the only one who knows?" I whisper, making sure to keep my voice so low I'm not sure even Oliver heard me at first.

He chuckles.

"It's more like Nat's the only one who doesn't know. Or doesn't care. I'm not really sure which."

Why wouldn't she care that Caleb was in love with her? Nat could be a little clueless, but she wasn't stupid. And she wasn't heartless.

Before I can ask Oliver what he might mean, the door Nat and Carrie disappeared behind slams open and Nat storms out. Carrie is close behind, her face looking withdrawn and forlorn. She doesn't try to stop Nat as she stomps straight for the front door and out.

"Parties over guys," Carrie calls out with a shrug. "You can all go home."

Oliver is on his feet, pulling me with him the moment the thought pops into my head to follow her.

"What the hell happened?" It's Caleb we almost run into when we exit the apartment, not Nat. She isn't anywhere to be seen and her car that is usually parked on the curb is gone. That was fast. Whatever happened really pissed her off, that's for sure.

"I have no idea," Oliver runs a hand through his hair. "We'll check the bar, you check the beach?"

Caleb nods and begins jogging in that direction, purpose written all over his face.

"Has this happened before?" I ask as we climb into Oliver's truck. He sighs as he cranks the ignition.

"There's a reason we all work together so well," he mutters. "None of us are as put together as we seem."

Chapter Fourteen

"She said she's been seeing this chick named Mary. How fucking cliche is that? Mary and Carrie. Sounds like the leads to a shitty TV show." Nat tosses back another shot. I'm not sure how many she's had. It's only been about twenty minutes since she left her apartment, but somehow she's already acting as if she's drunk half the bar.

"Nat, she isn't worth it," Caleb mutters. He doesn't look like he's just jogged all over town.

"She was the love of my life, Caleb," Nat snaps, motioning to the bartenders for another.

"The love of your life wouldn't treat you like that," he snaps back. There is a fire in his usual loving and humor filled eyes that I've never seen there before.

Oliver claps a hand on his shoulder and Caleb's head snaps over to look at him instead.

"You guys are acting weird," Nat finally mumbles. "I'm over tonight. I'm supposed to be getting married this week and instead I got my heart broken. Who the fuck is gonna dance with me?"

She stands with a wobble from her stool, catching herself on the bar. Oliver and Caleb seem to be locked into some kind of silent conversation and aren't paying her any attention. There is no way she's going onto the dance floor alone.

I've never been one for dancing - has to do a little something with the people - but I follow her anyway, stopping when she does in the center of the crowded dance floor. It's still early in the night, but it's a weekend and the bar is packed.

We move our bodies to two songs before Nat leans in close, her breath hot on my neck.

"Let's go outside," she shouts as if she isn't an inch away from me.

"I've never heard a better idea," I chuckle, this time towing her off the dance floor and towards the front door.

Once we break out into the evening warmth and lean against the brick wall, I notice what I hadn't in the club. Nat is crying. My breath stops in my throat. Nat always looks so put together, so perfect, so happy. Of course she is crying. Her life is crumbling around her. She'd be a psycho not to be upset.

So why am I so surprised?

Maybe because for so long it has felt as if I was the only one constantly falling apart. It seems like lately I might be the only one on the mend.

Am I? On the mend?

Yanking my thoughts back to the present, I pull Nat into a hug which she melts into, her sobs racking against my chest as she stoops down, bundling herself against me.

I'm not sure how long I hold her. I'm not sure how long we stand there as people pass by, shooting us questioning and sympathetic glances. I'm not sure how long it is, only that I am prepared to stand here all night if that is what she needs.

Caleb walks through the door first, followed by Oliver. Caleb's gaze immediately softens when it falls on Nat. If I have never once seen true love in my life, I have now. I'm not sure if the feeling is mutual, but Caleb would do anything for this girl.

"Come here," Caleb gently wraps his arms around her shoulders and pulls her to him. She slides easily from my grasp, sinking into him like water. "Nat, I got you." He strokes her hair as she sobs into his chest.

"I don't want to go home," she mumbles through her sobs.

"You don't have to," Caleb scoops her up into his arms and nods at us. Oliver has curled an arm around my waist. I'm not sure what to do now that someone else is taking care of Nat, so I let him hold me. "I've got her."

"Let us know when you're home," Oliver tells him.

"I love you guys!" Nat calls, her voice a mumbled slur as Caleb walks away.

"Love you too, Nat," Oliver calls back.

We don't talk much as we drive back to Nat's apartment. Oliver seems to know exactly what he's doing, so I follow his lead. He's in clean up mode. Her apartment is empty and dark when we arrive, no sign that anything has happened here besides the decorations and plastic cups strewn around the apartment.

Carrie's bags that were by the door are gone.

Oliver and I clean everything up and lock the door behind us, throwing two large garbage bags into the dumpster behind her complex before heading back to Oliver's truck on the curb.

"You guys have been a friend's a long time, huh?" I muse as we climb into his truck.

Oliver's laugh is low. He nods and turns the key in the ignition.

"Caleb and Chris moved here when they were about eight I think. Nat and I were already pretty inseparable at that point… or as inseparable as two eight year olds can be."

"So how did you end up so close with Chris and Caleb?"

"Tom knew my home life wasn't great. He would pack an extra lunch in one of their backpacks every day to give to me. In the other's bag there would be a clean change of clothes in case I hadn't been able to take a shower in a while."

I feel a twinge of pain in my heart for little Oliver. Visions of his tiny frame sitting in a small chair in the cafeteria with an empty tray in front of him, just hoping the big man who brings in those two twins might have thought of him today dance behind my eyes. I have to swallow hard to fight back tears. I don't say anything, allowing him to continue.

"It wasn't long before they were inviting me over for playdates. Neither of them would ever admit it, but I think Tom made them do it. I forced Nat to come along every time and quickly we were just always together. I don't really remember a time when it wasn't the four of us."

"Having a friend group like that must have been really comforting."

"It was." He nods. We still haven't pulled away from the curb, the truck idling gently around us. "And then it wasn't. And then it was again. Losing Chris really took a toll on us for a long time."

My jaw clenches and I blink away the tears still threatening the back of my eyes. What do I say to that? I bet? I can't imagine? I don't know what it's like to lose a friend to suicide. I wouldn't even begin to pretend that I do.

"I bet Chris was an amazing friend," I find myself saying instead.

Oliver's smile lights up his face, reaching his eyes in a way that makes butterflies assault my stomach. His mind is off in some memory as he begins speaking, that smile still on his lips.

"He was the best. Always the life of every party. He and Caleb could turn any bad day around with just a couple jokes. Them together was like nothing you've ever seen… of course, Chris had his struggles. Struggles I really only knew the depths of. I firmly believe there's no point in going back in time but if I could, the only thing I would ever change is that… I would tell Tom just how bad his mental health was. Instead of being so afraid we'd both be judged for it."

"I'm sure you did the best you could. You were only fifteen, right?"

He nods, his smile dimming a bit as he glances over at me.

"It wasn't until my fourth therapist, some quack in a basement two hours from here, that I actually believed his death wasn't my fault. Chris always did exactly what he wanted to do and if you told him no, it only fueled him further. He was a force."

"I wish I'd gotten to meet him," I whisper through my tear clogged throat, resting a hand on Oliver's where it's still just grasping the steering wheel.

My touch seems to jog something in Oliver. He looks over at me and his smile widens again. After a long moment, he starts the engine and the truck begins to crawl away from the curb.

"You would have loved him. Everybody did. We were just two fucked up teens who needed help. Unfortunately only one of us actually got it."

Oliver reaches across the cab and places his hand on my knee, giving it a squeeze. The conversation is over. I can only imagine how hard it is to talk about losing his best friend, but I'm glad that he did. I gnaw on my bottom lip for a moment as the town passes by us, staring off into the darkness. There's nothing that can fix the sadness I'm sure

Oliver is now feeling, but maybe there's something that can at least help him forget for a while.

"Let's go swimming," I finally say after a long moment of silence with only the soft hum of his engine to cradle us.

Oliver's smile is a blessing as he flashes it at me across the cab.

"Okay." His hand slides up to curl over my upper thigh, giving it a light squeeze. My entire body seems to melt at his touch. Fuck.

He parks in the spot reserved for him by his apartment and we get out. It is dark, the street lights and stars lighting up the sandy beach, just like the night we met. Only he's not already in the water this time and I'm not about to inappropriately invade his privacy.

Oliver strips down to his shorts, taking the journal I am now convinced is an extra limb out of his pocket and sitting it on his shirt on the beach.

Aunt Milly's is right across the road and I could easily go grab a bathing suit, but the beach is empty and it is dark, so instead I strip down to my underwear, dropping my clothes next to his.

Is Aunt Milly on the porch? Can she see us?

I realize as I let Oliver tug me closer to the lapping waves that I don't care if she sees us or not. I don't care if she's watching or if she tells my mom what she sees. I don't even care what she thinks.

An incredible feeling of relief washes over me at the realization. When was the last time I allowed myself to just do something without the fear of what someone else might think?

The water is cool but inviting. It was hot out today, and even in the evening air humidity still hangs around us. Oliver lets go of my hand and dives into the waves, disappearing for several long moments. His head pops up and back down again as his arms form powerful strokes through the water.

I wade up to my waist and stop, watching him and then the beach and the sky.

The summer is halfway over. How have I only known this place, these people… Olly…for a little over a month? And how is it all just supposed to end?

"You are so Goddamn beautiful." Oliver pulls me from my thoughts, his arms circling around me and pulling me to him.

He leans down and kisses me. His entire body is wet and slick, his hair and nose dripping salt water down on me. I giggle against his lips and he pulls back to look at me.

"What's so funny?"

What should I tell him? Lying to Oliver is beyond pointless. Since day one, he's been able to read me better than I can read myself. Even if he doesn't know what I'm thinking, he'll figure it out.

"You're getting me all wet." I finally laugh.

He brushes a hand across my cheek and runs it into my hair.

"We are standing in the ocean," He chuckles. "You're bound to get a little wet."

How does he do that to me? Just by looking into my eyes, he has the ability to completely undo me. I clear my throat and look away for a moment, trying to collect myself. I can feel an odd panic bubbling in my chest. Not quite the beginning of a panic attack, but something akin. What reason in this moment do I have to be panicked? I have no idea, but I also know that these things don't follow strict rules and I'd be a fool to think they do.

"Swim with me," I unravel myself from him and slip farther into the water, feeling him follow me.

I would follow Oliver anywhere, do anything, be anything. As I sink into the waves, feeling his body so close to mine doing the same thing, I wonder, what would Oliver do for me?

Even as I think the question, I know the answer is outside of my realm of comprehension. I've never felt like this for anyone before. What I thought was love for Leo wasn't even like compared to this. I've also never been cared for the way Oliver cares for me. It's a strange feeling and one I'm not sure how to embrace.

We swim for what feels like hours until my body is limp and tired. Oliver is clearly a much better swimmer than me. Once we wade out and begin towards Aunt Milly's, he's not even breathing hard as I lean against him for support.

"Do you want to see my room?" I ask him as we pause on the front steps. It's late and all of the lights inside are off. Aunt Milly is definitely in bed and even if she isn't… I'm an adult. And I'm not ready for the night to end.

"Sure." He kisses the top of my head and my insides turn to mush.

I'm not sure where the confidence is coming from as I lead him up the stairs towards the attic. My heart is hammering in my chest, my cheeks flushing deep red but I continue anyway.

I want to make Oliver happy. I want him to feel as amazing with me as I feel with him. I want to make him feel good.

We pause at the top of the steps and I gesture around, clopping over to the light switch.

"This is home." I say quietly with a shrug.

"Is everything okay?" Olly asks me, raising one eyebrow as he takes a step closer to me.

Shit. How does he do that? Read me so well before I've even said a word.

"Everything is great." I nod enthusiastically. "I'm just a little nervous."

"For what?" He asks, his eyebrows pulling together. He's left our dry clothes by the foot of the bed and is slowly closing the distance between us. We are dry enough from our walk back that the floor isn't getting too wet, but his hair is still dripping, covering his perfectly tan shoulders in little water droplets.

I gulp, trying my best to keep my eyes focused on his face as he wraps his arms around me. I can feel all of him pressed against me, his long length hard and pressing into my stomach. At the same moment I notice it, comprehension dawns on his face.

"We don't have to do anything," He tells me, kissing my temple. "Please don't be nervous. I don't want you to ever be nervous with me."

He misunderstood me. I'm not nervous because he's here in my bedroom or because I think he expects something from me.

"I'm nervous because I want to try something," I tell him, swallowing hard. "But I don't think I'll be any good at it."

"What do you want to try?" He asks.

I might be feeling a strange confidence, but I'm not feeling confident enough to actually say it. So instead, I take a step back and drop to my knees, tugging at the hem of his shorts as I do. They drop to his feet and it's only his wet boxers between me and him. They cling to his form, making the wetness between my legs intensify. I squirm to relieve the feeling and it only half works.

"Baby, if you want to try that," he says, his voice suddenly raspy, "don't doubt for a second that you'll be good at it. I come undone by just the thought of you. Anything you do is going to be enough."

Spurred on by his words, I take a deep breath and hook my fingers into the waistband of his boxers. I tug them down and focus on his feet as he steps out of his boxers and shorts, kicking them aside. Sliding my hands up his legs, I stop them on his upper thighs.

I had felt him against me. I knew his length and girth were impressive. I shift again as the feeling between my legs deepens.

Hesitantly, I wrap one hand around him and stroke. He moans and tilts his head back. Smiling at his reaction, I stroke him again, this time with more confidence. His stomach muscles tighten as he moans again.

I lick my lips and slowly take him into my mouth. I watched countless porn videos of girls giving blow jobs when I was in College, hoping to get the technique just right. Those girls always looked so beautiful and confident. I never felt that way when I gave head to Leo.

Now, I feel powerful.

I gag as he hits the back of my throat. Adjusting my position, I suck in a breath through my nose and begin to bob up and down.

"That feels so good, baby," He rasps.

Oliver wraps a hand in my hair and gently moves it back and forth with my head, applying light pressure to keep my pace even. There are tears forming at the corner of my eyes and my knees are beginning to sting, but I don't want to stop.

I want to make Oliver come.

"Baby," his voice is tight and breathless. "I am going to come," he warns me. I know he is warning me so I can stop but I don't want to.

I keep going, picking up the pace just a little and tightening my grip on his thighs.

"Stella," he moans and then his cock is pulsating and a warm, salty liquid is covering my tongue.

The moment he has finished, he pulls me to my feet and turns me towards the bed.

I giggle as he pushes me gently onto the mattress.

"Did I do good?" I ask.

"You did so good," He moans, crawling up the bed towards me and hooking his fingers into my underwear.

"I wanted to make you feel good," I admit.

"Did you like it?" He asks, pausing with his face an inch from my center. I squirm under his gaze. He knows exactly what he is doing to me.

"I liked how it made me feel." I decide. He smiles a wicked, sinful smile, and then continues to pull my bottoms down. "What are you doing?" I ask, though the answer is pretty obvious.

"I'm returning the favor." He says. "Probably twice for good measure."

Chapter Fifteen

A week has passed since the night of Nat's party. She showed up to work the next day, riding in Caleb's car, as if nothing had happened. Her mascara always seemed to be a bit smudged each time she returned from the bathroom, but otherwise, she seemed okay.

Beth hasn't reached out and won't answer any of my phone calls. Maybe I deserve this; being on the other end for a change. For so long, I ignored her. Maybe it's only right that she ignores me now.

"I'm off to the boutique," Aunt Milly kisses the top of my head where I am sitting on the front porch, a mug of coffee in one hand and a slice of toast in the other. "Have a good day off sweetie."

"Thanks, Aunt Milly," I talk around my bite and give her a small wave as she pads lightly down to her car, gets in and drives off.

She has such a quaint, quiet life here. Even with the bustling tourists streets lurking only blocks away, there is something so calming about living here. I let myself imagine for just a moment what it might feel like to live here for real. Not just for the summer with a time stamp on it, but year round. To know this was home.

I bet it's a beautiful feeling.

I don't notice Oliver is jogging across the street towards me until he's almost to the porch.

"Good morning, beautiful," he jogs up the steps and brushes a kiss on my lips. I smile as he sinks down onto the swing beside me. "Caleb is having a little party tonight. Are we going to see you or should I tell Caleb I can't make it?"

"Are those the only two options?" I laugh.

He nods.

"Yep. Where you go, I go." He shifts and I feel that forever present notebook in his cargo shorts pocket rubbing against my leg.

My own is sitting beside us on the side table, reminding me I still have two bullet points to add. Somehow, it feels scary to add them. Like they are too final. Too finished.

"Can I ask you something?" I shift the coffee mug in my hands, focusing on the warmth. How does Oliver have the ability to make me so nervous yet so calm at the same time? My body is constantly at war with itself when he is around. It's a feeling I will never grow tired of. As if I am a live wire.

"Anything," he squeezes my knee.

"What are your ten? On your list?"

"Didn't you read it already?" He wiggles his eyebrows and I flush deep red. He's said over and over that he's not mad about the way we met, yet somehow I still feel guilty over it. It feels as if it were a lifetime ago and not a mere month.

"I only read the first two."

He digs the notebook out of his pocket, but doesn't hand it right over.

"How about a deal? You show me yours, I'll show you mine?" His eyes dart to my own notebook laying within reaching distance.

I shake my head so fast my vision blurs. He cocks an eyebrow.

"Why not?"

"It's not done yet," I swallow hard. "I only have eight points. I don't want you to see it until it's done."

His expression has dropped slightly, a disappointment reaching his eyes, but he nods and hands me his own.

"Okay. Here, keep it today while I'm at work. There's several lists in there. Read them all."

"Olly-" I start, but he squeezes my thigh again, the smile returning to his lips.

"I want you to know all of me, Stella. This book is honestly the quickest way. It's like a window into my soul," he kisses me, standing and walking for the steps again. "I'm covering a morning shift at the center, but I'll see you tonight?"

I nod.

"Have a good day!" I call after him as he jogs across the road. He flashes me a smile and a little wave. His hair is loose, bouncing on his tanned shoulders as he runs. His tattoos glisten in the sun, his freckled arms moving smoothly at his sides.

I try to wait to open the journal until he's completely out of sight. My fingers itch towards it, intrigue taking over the little patience I have. I know that it's not fair of me to be so excited to read what he's written when I can't find it in me to share my own with him. I know I shouldn't look and I should just give it back to him. That or suck it up and let him read mine.

I know all of these things.

That doesn't mean I am going to listen to them.

If I've learned one thing this summer, it's that I am an incredibly selfish person.

Oliver has just rounded the first corner in his truck, his blinker announcing his exit from view, when I flip open the book. The first page is stiff and water stained, each bullet point written over and over with pen so many times that the ink is bleeding through the thick paper to the other side. According to the date, he would have written this list in Highschool.

I swallow over a lump in my throat and flip through the pages until I reach the last one - the one he wrote this summer. I'm not quite ready for the others yet, I don't think. Oliver is such a whole person to me; at least, the Oliver that I know.

Seeing the hurt that he felt at such a young age spelt out on paper like I know I am going to when I flip back is something I need a bit to prepare myself for.

The list that I already got a peek of flops open on my knee.

I read the entire thing in one go, forcing myself to continue scanning the page instead of stopping to reflect on each one. The farther down I go, the thicker the lump in my throat is and the more apparent the tears threatening to spill from my eyes are.

1. *Learn how to smile without faking it*
2. *Finally finish that tattoo. Fuck, it's been 3 years.*
3. *Listen to Caleb's advice more. It's actually pretty good.*
4. *Listen to your own advice. That's pretty good too.*
5. *Gather up the courage to talk to Stella.*
6. *Get Stella to trust you.*
7. *Sleep more. Fuck, I'm exhausted.*
8. *Go swimming more. I miss it.*
9. *Stop being so afraid and just write 10. Fuck.*
10. *Tell Stella you are in love with her.*

Until next time - Oliver

I read the list once, and then again, and then a third time, my jaw dropping open farther with each read. Oliver is in love with me.

Oliver is in love with me.

No matter how many times the words rattle around in my brain, I can't seem to make them make sense.

"Stella!" Nat is jogging towards me from her car parked directly in front of the steps. I didn't even see her maneuvering it into the parallel spot amidst the bustling street. She's wearing a bright pink dress, her hair curled down her back in thick waves. She doesn't work today either, but Caleb does. I know she's been staying at their place this week, too upset to go back to her own apartment, but Oliver hasn't had much to say about it.

I shove both his journal and mine behind my back, hoping she didn't see.

"Hey, Nat." I plaster on the biggest smile I can manage, hoping it doesn't look too dazed.

Oliver is in love with me. My heart could explode.

Her own expression is far off, as if her mind isn't quite here either. But she does look excited, if not a tad bit nervous. She's wringing her hands and biting down on her bottom lip. I force thoughts of Oliver to the back of my head and sit up straighter, giving her my full attention.

"I need to tell you something and you have to promise not to hate me," she says, biting down on her lower lip as she settles on the seat across from me.

"I could never hate you," I laugh, the sound shaky and not because I don't mean it. I could never hate Nat. I'm pretty sure she could admit to committing murder and I'd find a way to believe she had her reasons. My laugh wavers because after she tells me whatever thing might make me hate her, it'll be my turn to divulge my own secret. What if she chooses to hate me?

She sucks in a deep breath, closes her eyes, and then spews out the words so fast I almost don't catch them.

"I slept with Caleb. Three times. It was amazing. It was beyond amazing, it was world altering good sex, Stella, and I don't know what to do because he is in love with me and I just can't be right now. I am a God awful person. Please, please tell me you hate me. I need somebody to hate me because Caleb keeps saying he doesn't and that just isn't fair. He should. He should hate me."

When she's finished her eyes flash open and she's breathing heavy, her eyes round and concerned.

I'm not sure what I was expecting, but it was not that. I bite down on my lower lip, taking a moment to let what she said sink in.

"Do you want advice or for me to listen?" I finally ask.

"I don't know."

"If it makes you feel any better, Oliver loves me and as much as I love him back, I know we could never work. I am going to have to break his heart. So maybe we are both terrible people. Maybe we both deserve to be hated."

Nat stands from her seat and instead of remaining standing, she sinks down next to me, so close we are basically on top of one another. She wraps her arms around me and rests her head on my shoulder. I allow myself to breathe, closing my eyes for a moment as I feel her against me.

"Why do we both believe so deeply we aren't worthy of good things?" She finally mutters.

The stillness in the air is heavy. I am sure there are people talking, laughing, walking by the house. I am sure the waves are hitting the beach, a seagull is probably shrieking. But all I hear is the silence.

I'm not sure if she's waiting for an answer or not, but I don't have one to give her. I know why I'm not good enough. I am selfish. I am needy and heartless. Oliver deserves a person who is kind and good like him. He doesn't deserve someone like me.

Nat deserves all that is good. She is light and beauty and even though sure, she fucked up, that doesn't change the fact that she deserves the world.

I wish she could see that.

But I don't tell her, because she's not in the place to hear it and I'm not in the place to tell her. We are both broken and sometimes broken things just can't be fixed.

*   *   *

I want to throw my phone across the room the moment it begins ringing.

I was just about to open up Oliver's journal, now that I am once again alone on the front porch. The urge to thumb through each page and read every word is so strong, I almost ignore my phone.

Beth's name blinks on the screen, mocking me.

I sigh heavily and sit his journal back down, picking up the phone instead.

"Hey." I say, as if this is just a casual call. As if the weight of our worlds aren't holding onto it. As if she hasn't ignored my calls. As if everything is okay.

"Hey." She replies, just as airy and light and somehow still completely forced.

"I want to start off by saying that I am so sorry for the way I left Maine," She is talking quickly, trying to get everything out before I interrupt her, so I bite my tongue. She deserves for me to listen at the very least. We've both fucked up. "Leo suggested it and it just felt…easier. But I know it was wrong. I went to the police over Luke. He has a court date. I left Leo. He was good for me in the moment but I need to be alone right now. Stella, I am really trying here, and it's not easy. I could really use my best friend. Not the girl who I barely know, but the girl who got me through High School. I need her."

Air is stuck in my throat.

What if that girl no longer exists?

What if she's asking for something that is impossible? But she doesn't need to hear that right now. She needs comfort. She needs me.

"I'm here Beth," I force the words out. "I am so proud of you and everything is going to be okay. I am here."

I wonder if I'm the only one who can hear my voice waver, wondering if the words I'm speaking are the truth or a beautiful lie.

Chapter Sixteen

"You know you could come inside," Caleb is leaning against the door frame to their apartment as I pace a line in the sand just outside.

I shake my head, ringing my hands together.

"If I go inside I am going to lose the nerve I am barely holding onto right now."

"You know Oliver is in love with you right? You could spit in his face, call him an asshole and he'd still be in love with you. Why are you so nervous?"

"Was I the only one who didn't know?" I shriek, throwing my hands up in the air.

Caleb laughs. It's a tired laugh. He looks so tired. He's crumpling his hat in his hands, pushing the bill together and then shaking it out over and over. For what feels like the hundredth time since I met him, I wonder why he hasn't replaced the darn thing. Yet somehow Caleb wouldn't be Caleb without it, dirt stains, rips and all.

Is everyone in this little town secretly holding it all together with thread? Part of me wishes I could go back to before I moved here for the summer, before the curtain was pulled back, when I thought everyone here was happy and perfect. Another part of me knows that doing that would mean I never would have met any of these people - Oliver - and that's not something I would ever sacrifice.

"The only one who knew what?" Oliver's voice is close behind me.

I twirl to find him standing in the sand, a lunch box in one hand and his truck keys dangling from the other.

Caleb laughs and dips inside.

"See you two later," He chuckles, closing the door behind him.

Just like this morning, the world seems to silence for the two of us. I can see the families on the beach, I can see the waves crashing against the sand. I can even see the birds swooping in for food scraps. Cars are whizzing by on the busy street. Our tiny town is alive and in a bustle today, but none of it matters.

"You love me." The words fall from my mouth, foreign and heavy.

"So you read my journal." Oliver chuckles, sitting his lunch box down and stuffing his keys into his pocket. I want to throw myself at him, wrap my arms around him… I want to be close to him.

But instead I am frozen in place.

"Just the one list."

"I love you, Stella." He shrugs. The words fall so easily from his mouth, it's as if he's been saying it forever. "I've loved you since the moment I met you. I know that sounds corny and stupid but… it would be worse to say what I actually think."

"Which is?" My heart is going to beat directly out of my chest if I'm not careful.

"I've loved you since before I met you."

Tears are prickling the edge of my eyes. I want so badly to shout, to tell him I love him too. I want to tell him I am in love with him, that no matter what, we are going to work out. I want to tell him that I will try my hardest to be the person he deserves even though I know I'm not.

Instead, I force myself to look away from him and sprint up the sidewalk to Aunt Milly's, ignoring his calls as I run. His voice fades into the noises of the beach, and I slam the door shut. I'm not sure which is louder, the waves drowning out my sobs, or my sobs drowning out the waves.

*   *   *

"Stella." Aunt Milly is at the foot of the attic steps, her voice calling softly up to me. She's been calling to me for hours. My crying stopped a bit ago, but she still doesn't dare intrude. "Honey, can I come up?"

"Go ahead." I call back.

"Oliver's been knocking at the door every twenty minutes," She says gently as she walks into my room. Her hair is in braids and she's wearing a long green sundress. I wish to be as carefree and gentle as her one day. "And I see he's been calling you." She nods towards my phone which is currently lit up, displaying ten missed calls.

I sniffle, tucking his journal under my pillow next to mine.

I've been reading it. Each and every list is now carved into the back of my eyelids. He's had such a rough life. He's so broken. Just like me. And he loves me.

"I can't, Aunt Milly." I finally say.

She sits on the edge of my bed.

"You can't what?"

"I can't believe a guy like him would love a person like me."

To my surprise, she smiles.

"Do you love him back, Stella?"

I nod so quickly, her smile widens.

"Of course you don't know how he could love you. When you're truly in love, you never feel as if you could be good enough. But you are, honey."

I'm not sure what to say. I'm feeling that a lot lately, like other people have so much more to say than I do. Maybe I'm just not used to being the one asking for help. Maybe I've never allowed myself to be.

"I remember the first time I fell in love," Aunt Milly muses. "I don't think I've ever really been in love since. We were in High School, he was kind and handsome and wise beyond his years. He would have moved worlds for me and I was head over heels for him."

"What happened?"

"I was too scared to jump," She shrugs simply. "Your grandparents got divorced around the same time and your mom and I moved to Vermont with your grandfather. He waited for me even as he went off to college, but I was too scared to make a move. Now it's too late. Stella, life will so easily just happen to you if you let it. I was so proud of you when you decided to come out here for the summer. Do you know why?"

I shake my head.

"Because you weren't allowing anything to just happen. You made a choice. You did something. And even if it turns out to be wrong, at least you tried."

"I thought you didn't approve of Oliver."

She shakes her head and smiles. It feels as if that conversation we had was ages ago. Everything feels like a lifetime ago and a split second at the same time.

"I want you to be happy, Stella. If Oliver makes you happy, I want you to jump. Don't be so scared of getting hurt that you stay stuck. Don't be like me."

I laugh, a broken, half laugh.

"Aunt Milly, all I've ever wanted is to be like you."

"Well," She nudges me softly in the side, a light and beautiful smile settled on her lips. "Be like me in all ways but your love life. Go get the boy, Stella. For both of us."

*　　　*　　　*

1. *Wear more skirts. I like skirts.*
2. *Stop being so afraid of everything.*
3. *Stop falling for Oliver. You Idiot.*
4. *Stop being such a shitty fucking friend.*
5. *Stop thinking about Leo. It's in the past.*
6. *Figure out how not to push everyone away (good luck)*
7. *Look at yourself the way Oliver looks at you.*
8. *Convince yourself you are not always the problem.*

I stare at my list, my fingers brushing over the pages as my heart beats wildly in my chest. Right now, I know only two things to be certain.

One. I know the last two items on my list.

Two. I need to see Oliver. Right now.

I uncap my pen and begin scribbling.

9. *Stay in Maine you coward.*
10. *You love Oliver. Allow yourself to.*

I don't even allow myself to look any longer at the words before I'm stuffing the book back under my pillow with Oliver's, pushing my feet into my sandals, and running down the steps.

Aunt Milly only glances up from her book in the kitchen, a smile on her lips.

"Good luck." She calls after me as the porch door creaks and closes behind me.

I am half way across the street, running towards Oliver's house, when I notice the people and the music. And then I remember. Caleb was having a party tonight. That conversation feels like forever ago and somehow, doesn't even matter.

I continue across the street, only a tad slower. I don't even bother to pause at the door which is wide open. The living room and kitchen are packed with bodies, but I don't even get to notice a single face before a cold hand is wrapping around my arm and pulling me into the bathroom.

I squeal but quickly shut up once Nat closes the door and crosses her arms over her chest.

"Are you here to break Oliver's heart? If you are, girl, I support you in what you need but just let me know because I gotta get the bandaids and scotch ready." Her eyes are so wide I'm afraid they're going to bug out of her head.

"Nat, I love you," I place my hands on her shoulders. "But if you don't get out of my way right now, I am going to scream at you."

Her big eyes and scowl turn quickly into a wide smile. She bounces on her heels.

"So you aren't going to tell him to fuck off?"

"No!" I throw my hands in the air. "But if you don't move I'm going to lose my nerve and do nothing. Where is he?"

"His room I think." She steps to the side, wiggling her eyebrows at me. Right before I slip out the door, she grabs my arm and squeezes. "You do deserve him, Stella. You're a good person."

Swallowing over the lump in my throat that causes, I quickly weave my way through the bodies clogging their home and head straight for his bedroom.

The door is closed but I don't bother knocking.

I open it and slide inside, closing it and locking it behind me before pausing to see if he's even in the room. He is standing by the head of his bed with his shirt half on, in the middle of changing. When the lock clicks he pauses, staring at me, arms still over his head. I'm almost sure that if I looked at the clock on the wall, the hands would have stopped moving.

"Stella-"

"Stop." I hold up a hand, shaking my head. "Please let me say this or I never will."

He finishes pulling down his shirt and then stands completely still. He is beautiful. Perfect.

Clasping my hands tightly together, I suck in a deep breath and then explode with every held in thought, not even pausing between words to breathe. I need to say this and I need to say all of it. Especially with the way Oliver is staring at me right now. His eyes are so warm and trusting, if I don't say it now, I'll collapse into him and allow myself to just pretend he already knows.

"I have felt as if something is wrong with me my entire life. When I was little, I was too loud. In High School I was too big, too much of everything and not enough at the same time somehow. Once I graduated I couldn't do enough for my parents, I couldn't do the one thing that they wanted me to do. I couldn't just be the good little daughter and go to college and make them happy. My entire life, I've just never been what anyone wanted me to be," I suck in a deep, shaky breath. Oliver is still staring at me, as still as a statue. Is he holding his breath too?

"Until I met you. You don't make me feel like I have to be anything or do anything. You make me feel as if I'm enough exactly the way I am. Selfish, self absorbed…none of it matters. My flaws don't matter when I'm with you. And that scares the absolute shit out of me."

I take a single step, closing the distance only a little. Oliver remains totally still. I take another step and then another. There's now only a foot between us.

"You scare the shit out of me. You are so real and kind and perfect. You are the kind of person who deserves the world, Oliver, and I know in my heart I can never give that to you."

"Stella-"

"No!" I hold up a hand. "I'm not done."

I take another step, closing the distance completely and grab his hands in mine. They are so warm, so welcoming. I hold them for a moment before letting them drop and pressing my body against his instead. I wrap my arms up and around his neck, pressing a single kiss to the line of his jaw.

"I have struggled with feeling inadequate my entire life. I am done. You scare me because you make me believe that maybe I am worth something. But mostly you scare me because when I love something, I'm not capable of loving it in halves. When I love I am all in. Oliver, I am so in love with you it hurts. And I am done trying to convince myself that I'm not."

It's as if there was an elephant on my chest and it's just now decided to stand up. I breathe a sigh of relief and finally allow myself to crane my neck up to look into his face. He's smiling, his eyes glinting with a happiness I can feel radiating throughout his entire body.

"Say it again." He mutters.

"I love you, Oliver." I stretch up onto my toes and brush a kiss over his lips.

It's soft and quick. I've no sooner pulled back then Oliver's wrapping his arms around my waist and pressing me to him, his lips finding mine like a starving man finally getting a meal.

I laugh against his lips as he picks me up off my feet. I circle my legs around his waist, tangling my hands into his perfectly shaggy hair. There is so much of him and not enough of me. I need to be breathing him, consumed by him, surrounded by him.

"Oliver," I moan against his lips.

"Yes baby?"

"Tell me you love me." I groan, trailing kisses down his jaw and back up.

He chuckles, spinning us so my back is facing the bed and gently throwing me into the covers. I squirm under his gaze, taking in all of him as he takes in all of me.

"I love you, Stella." His grin should be illegal.

My heart is hammering in my chest, a familiar tingle between my legs threatening to take over my senses. I have been beyond confused these past twenty four hours, torn between what is right and what is wrong, but in this moment I know exactly what I want and I am done fighting it.

"Oliver." I whisper, forcing the words up as they threaten to slide back down.

He leans over me, the bed sinking slightly as his fists hold him up beside my head. His lips are inches from mine. He is so close yet not nearly close enough.

"I want you." I whisper. "All of you. Now."

He closes the inches between us, kissing me with a hunger I return. When he pulls back, his eyes are full of a lust I can feel in my bones.

"You have me baby."

Chapter Seventeen

I will never get tired of staring at Oliver. He is perfect. As he reaches for the hem of his shirt, I feel my chest tightening with anticipation. I have seen him shirtless countless times yet I am still giddy with glee at the thought of seeing it again.

"I am a patient man. I would have waited years for you, Stella. But I'd be lying if I said I haven't wanted this since the day we met." He stops and leans back down, his hands tracing a path along my curves. He tugs the hem of my shirt up, exposing my soft stomach. He kisses from my bra down to my shorts and back up. "You Stella, are beautiful. Perfect in every way."

Oliver's voice is intoxicating. I could drown in it and die happy.

He is lavishing me in attention, his hands roaming over every inch of me as if he is trying to memorize my body. As much as I am enjoying it, I am also quivering with anticipation. I need more.

"Oliver, take your shirt off."

He laughs, a chuckle so low and sexy it sends waves of pleasure coursing through me.

"I just put it on."

"I think I might actually pass out if you aren't naked in twenty seconds." I laugh. It was supposed to sound confident and sexy, but it came out as a pant and didn't sound either.

"Time me." He winks as he stands up. I begin to count as he quickly tugs off each article of clothing. The counting calms my nerves and by the time I've reached 0 and he's standing in only his boxers, I am at least breathing closer to normal than I was.

"I made it." He winks.

"You missed one."

"You first." His fingers work the button on my shorts, going slow and easy. He's giving me plenty of time to tell him to stop.

I'm not going to.

There isn't a universe in which I would want Oliver to take his hands off my body. Personally, I think even though they are brushing my stomach with each movement, they aren't close enough.

"Are you sure about this?" He pauses as he hooks his thumbs into my shorts.

Instead of answering, I sit up and in one swift motion strip my shirt from my head. Without even thinking, I reach behind my back and unclasp my bra, throwing that to meet my shirt on the floor. Oliver's eyes roam over me, burning hot with desire. A desire I feel in my own stomach.

"I need this, Oliver."

As if telling me "say less", Oliver pushes me back into the pillows and pulls off my last article of clothing. My pink panties don't even make it to the floor, sitting beside us in a ball on the bed instead.

Before I can laugh at how odd it is my brain picked up on that one fact, Oliver is between my legs and I am moaning his name.

His tongue works over me, his hands holding my thighs apart. I wind my hands into his hair, my own head pushing back into the pillows. He's only been between my legs a few minutes but I can already feel my legs shaking.

"Oliver, stop." I moan.

He does, reluctantly. His eyes are gleaming as he looks up at me over my stomach, licking his lips. I could orgasm from just that look alone.

"I need you inside me." I rasp.

"What, you don't want me to finish?"

I shake my head.

"Now, Oliver."

I have never been this demanding before. It feels electrifying. I feel powerful and sexy. Oliver kneels up between my legs. He's looking at me as if I am the most attractive woman he has ever seen. I am drunk on love and power, high with it, and I never want to come down.

The bed dips slightly as he steps to the side, pulling off his boxers in one swift motion.

My breath catches in my throat in a way I'm not proud of. I've seen him naked before but something about tonight feels different.

Oliver naked is something made of dreams. Tattoos cover almost every inch of his body, dark art enhancing his tanned and freckled figure.

Before I can really comprehend what he's doing, he's reaching into his bedside stand and grabbing a small package. A condom.

I follow him with my eyes as he moves back onto the bed. He spreads my legs apart, kneeling back between them as he rolls the condom down over his impressive length.

"If at any point you want me to stop-"

"Oliver, please. I will tell you if I change my mind. I need you. Now."

The smile that slides onto his lips should be illegal.

"I'll go slow. Breath."

He kisses along my stomach, up and over each breast, trailing a path that ends at my lips. As his lips cover mine, I feel him pressing at my entrance, and then he is filling me.

I gasp as the foreign feeling overwhelms my body. There is a slight pinch but it is gone just as quickly, taken over by the fullness I feel there instead. Oliver pauses for a moment at the sound, assessing my face to make sure I'm not in pain. When he's satisfied, he kisses me again before thrusting a little deeper.

He continues to push slowly until he is buried completely inside me, pulling his face back to look at me.

"You okay?"

Taking a deep, shaky breath, I nod. As his hips shift, another feeling entirely begins to take over.

I was already wet, already practically panting for him, but this is different. This feeling vibrates through me, begging for more. Begging to feel more.

"Better than okay." I assure him.

"That's it baby. Take it for me."

Oh fuck. Dirty talk from Oliver is something I wasn't prepared for. Not now.

As he begins to move, my nails dig into his back. I am trying to hold on as long as I can. I don't want this to end, but I can feel myself beginning to let go. A wonderful warmth is starting in my center, threatening to spill across my entire body and I don't want to stop it.

"Olly," I gasp. I'm not sure what I was going to say because suddenly, I am overcome with pleasure. I have orgasmed before. At my own touch and at Olly's, but this is something else entirely. This is bliss.

"Come for me, Stella."

Just as his words whisper into my ear, I feel his entire body tense as his own release rushes alongside mine.

He kisses me twice before rolling off of me. He's only on his back beside me for a second before he's pulling me to his chest, kissing my hair and wrapping the comforter from his bed around us both.

"That was amazing," I whisper into his chest.

"I love you, Stella." He whispers back.

For once, I don't question myself as I answer. For once, I am sure that I am deserving and he is deserving and we are made for each other. For just this moment, everything is perfect. For this moment, nothing is going to ruin us.

"I love you, Olly."

For now, we have this. And for now, this is enough.

*   *   *

"Do you think he's the one?" Beth asks, her tone lighthearted and airy. It's nice to hear her finally at ease. She's been staying with Daven and Malory, trying to get back on her feet as she figures out pregnancy and court hearings. At least she's safe. I know my brother won't let anything happen to her and she knows it too.

She's not the only one who's seen a change.

It's been a week since my night with Olly. It was as if that night flipped a switch.

It had nothing to do with the sex.

The moment I decided I was enough, suddenly I was. I called Beth the next day and we've been talking at length each day since.

Nat and I are sitting in my car after a long shift, waiting for Caleb to come out from counting his tips. It's been awkward with the two of them, but they are choosing to act as if nothing happened so I go along with it.

Beth is on speaker and Nat is practically jumping out of the passenger seat with glee.

"She does!" Nat squeals.

I roll my eyes.

"I love him," I admit, shrugging. It's the first time I've said it out loud to anyone but him or Aunt Milly.

Just as I say it, an incoming call beeps over Beth's name. Aunt Milly's name flashes on the screen.

"I gotta let you go, Beth. Talk to you later?"

"Yeah. I think Daven is ordering chinese. I'll call you after dinner."

We hang up and Nat scoots down in her seat as she sees Caleb nearing the car. She pulls out her phone, scrolling through it as if she has been this whole time. Again, I roll my eyes, pressing answer on my phone.

"Hey Aunt Milly."

"Hi honey. Are you on your way home?"

My brow wrinkles in confusion. I've lived with her for almost two months now and she's never questioned where I am. Especially when she knew I was at work.

"Just waiting for Caleb," I tell her as he opens the door and slides in.

"What about me?" He asks.

I wave a hand at him as Nat rolls her eyes and slides even further down in her seat. He just shrugs and looks out the window into the dark night. We closed the restaurant late tonight. It's a Saturday. Normally, we'd all be going down to the bar.

Tonight, we all agreed we were way too exhausted.

"There's someone here waiting for you," she says, a light laugh following the sentence.

My brow scrunches further.

"Huh?"

I don't have friends. The only ones I have are in the car with me. Olly wouldn't be at my Aunt's house when he knew I was working late…right?

My heart begins to thud in my chest.

"Aunt Milly-" I start.

"We'll see you when you get here," She says in a sing-song tone, then the call ends.

"Olly is a dead man." I groan.

"What'd he do now?" Caleb asks from the back seat. Nat even perks up, waiting for my answer.

"I think he's at my Aunt's house."

"Death row for him," Nat chuckles.

Neither of them would understand. If they would get their heads out of their asses and admit they were made for each other, everyone would be on board. Despite the latest discussion I had with my Aunt and her reassurance that she just wants me to be happy, I can't help but think back to the first day I was here.

"Don't even think about it," she had said as Oliver and Caleb had stood with a group of friends around a bike rack by the ocean.

Oliver wouldn't have walked right into her house knowing I wasn't going to be there, right? He knows how she feels about him. He knows she doesn't approve. As soon as I think about it, I know for a fact that is exactly what he did. Olly doesn't like gray areas.

I drive ten over the speed limit the entire way back from the diner. It's a quick trip anyway, but one I cut the time of in half with the way my heart is beating in my chest. I park on the curb and cut the engine.

"See you," Caleb jumps from the car and jogs across the street before the headlights have even dimmed.

Nat crosses her arms over her chest, glaring at his back as it disappears into the darkness. She's still staying with them, several weeks after her breakup with Carrie. She's sleeping on the couch and insists her and Caleb have gone back to just being friends. I have my own opinions on the entire thing, but I have chosen to keep my mouth firmly shut. They are both my friends and I am not willing to sacrifice either friendship for the other.

"He acts as if he isn't in love with me."

"You turned him down, Nat," I say gently.

She huffs, shaking her head.

"I know. He could at least look at me."

I pat her arm without saying anything else, because what do you say? I've never been engaged and cheated on. I've never slept with my best friend knowing nothing was ever going to happen between us.

So instead of advice, I offer the only thing I have. My presence.

"I'll see you later, Stell." She sighs. "Love you."

"Love you," I tell her. I don't get out of the car until she's safely made it across the road and disappeared into the house. Only then do I get out myself and begin up the steps towards the porch where I can already see Olly on the swinging bench and Aunt Milly sitting cross legged in the chair opposite him.

They both look serious.

Shit.

"How was work, honey?" Aunt Milly turns to face me as I walk up the steps. Her smile doesn't look fake or forced. That's a good sign.

I lean down and allow her to give me a quick hug before I settle down onto the bench beside Olly. He immediately wraps his arm around my shoulder and I lean into him.

"It was good. Busy." I tell them both. "What's going on here?"

"I told you she'd be suspicious." Aunt Milly laughs, wagging a finger at Olly. "The poor guy just wanted to go for a swim with you."

I narrow my eyes at him. He knew I was at work.

"I do," He agreed. "I also wanted to formally meet your Aunt too. Is that wrong?"

"No." I shake my head, all but staring at him. I'm continually amazed by him. "Not at all."

"I'll leave you two," Aunt Milly stands, stretching and facing the ocean. Her hair whips her face. There is a storm rolling in. It will be here by tomorrow, leaving a chill in the air tonight. "Goodnight honey."

"Night Aunt Milly."

She flashes Olly a smile, one full of the conversation I'll never get to hear, and then disappears into the house.

"What was that really about?" I playfully punch his shoulder the moment we are truly alone.

He laughs.

"Honestly. I wanted to go for a swim."

"Right." I roll my eyes.

"Milly had some misconceptions about me. I needed to clear them up. For our sake."

Oh. Misconceptions about what? I know there are things about Olly's past I don't know. I know Aunt Milly has her reasons for thinking badly of him. But none of that has mattered to me since he told me about Chris. Even now, I can't think of a single thing he could tell me he did that would be a deal breaker for me.

"Let me go change," I say instead of asking any questions or even acknowledging I heard what he said.

I jog through the dark house, up to the attic. Stripping out of my dirty, food smelling clothes, I toss on the first bathing suit my fingers brush. It's a blue string bikini that I've never worn in public. It's night time, dark out, and Olly isn't public.

Just before jogging back down the steps, I pause at my pillow and grab both Olly's journal and my own.

"These are for you." I tell him as I come back out onto the porch, shoving both towards him.

"Are you sure?" He asks, noticing mine on top.

I nod.

"It's not much. Just a couple little lists. But you deserve to see them. I read all of yours."

"Only if you want me to, Stella."

"I do," I assure him. "Come on, let's go swimming."

I don't want to talk about the journals or my Aunt, or even work. I grab his hand and tug him across the road, squealing as we dart out in front of a slowly moving van. Probably full of tourists. The season is coming to an end. Fall is nipping at our heels and I want to savor every bit of summer that I have left.

"Wait for me," Olly chuckles, pulling his shirt off and wrapping the journals in it, plopping the bundle down in the sand far away from the crashing waves, before following me into them.

The water is cold. My body immediately breaks out in goosebumps, sending shivers down my spine and into my hairline. I ignore the feeling.

"I don't ever want to leave here," I laugh as I come up for air. Water drops down my face, from the ends of my hair, from my eyelashes. My body is growing numb from the cold. I don't care. This is living.

"Then don't," Olly wraps his arms around me, pulling me to him. We are both soaked, our skin sliding as our feet slip on the sand, the waves pushing us around.

I stretch up and kiss him, closing my eyes and savoring the moment.

"Maybe I won't," I finally laugh against his lips.

There are moments in life when you are so sure of something, you would bet anything on it. This was one of those moments. I knew without a doubt that Olly and I were meant to be together, and I knew there was nothing that could make me question that.

If I had the chance to go back in time and tell the girl smiling and laughing in the ocean that night what was about to happen the next day, would I?

Probably. It would be the fair thing to do.

Being blindsided the way I was can only lead to one thing - panic. And panic makes us do stupid things.

Chapter Eighteen

"I'm freezing," I gasp, my teeth chattering as we run for the house. Oliver's hand is in mine, tugging me along as our feet slip in the sand.

He laughs, yanking the door open and we dart into the warmth of his apartment. All of the lights are off and no one is up. Caleb is more than likely asleep in his room or maybe he decided to go to the bar after all. Nat's chest is rising and falling slowly, curled up under a bundle of blankets on the couch. She stirs a bit when the door closes, nestling farther into the cushions before her body stills again.

Olly holds a finger to his lips as I giggle, following him to his bedroom. We leave a trail of water behind us leading straight to his bathroom where he grabs us both a towel.

Instead of giving me one to dry myself off with, he begins to gently pat me down, wiping the droplets from my body as if I'm made of glass.

"Have I told you how perfect you are?" He murmurs, brushing the towel over my stomach. As he leans down to dry my legs, his wet hair brushes the inside of my thighs and I squirm.

"I think you've mentioned it." I whisper, my voice barely audible. How odd it is to think that now when he says it, I actually believe it.

Resting on his knees he drops the towel to the floor and kisses the inside of my thigh. I feel his tongue flick out to catch a water droplet and I fight the urge to rub my thighs together.

No matter how many times Oliver pulls my bottoms down, I think I will always turn a bright shade of red.

"Put your leg on my shoulder." He says once my bottom half is naked and directly in his face.

I do as he asks and he immediately begins to worship me, his tongue gently probing over my clit as his hands rub over my thighs.

I lean back against the shower door, moaning as I feel my body beginning to weaken. His hands tighten on my legs, holding me up as he continues. I don't think he'll stop until I'm a puddle.

Finding the will buried deep in my toes, I gently push his head away and drop my leg. He looks up, a slight disappointment on his face.

"I want to come with you inside me." I tell him and the look quickly dissolves into excitement.

He stands and pulls me into the bedroom. I strip my top off before climbing into the bed and pulling the covers over us. The warmth of the blankets is inviting, but not as inviting as Oliver's warmth as he crawls in beside me and pulls me against him.

We kiss for so long I finally have to pull back for air, our semi dry bodies intertwined so tightly I don't ever want to let go.

When we do pull back, Olly's hands begin to roam over my body, tracing my curves as if he is memorizing them. One drops between my legs and begins to rub my sensitive clit, eliciting a moan from me so unexpected I giggle.

"What's so funny?" He laughs a breathy laugh against my shoulder, following it with a kiss.

Instead of answering, I roll onto my side and take him by surprise, climbing on top of him. Stradling Oliver is another level of powerful.

"Is this okay?" I ask, reaching between us to guide him to my opening.

"More than okay." He assures me, grabbing my hips.

A wave of unexpected nerves hit me as he does and I pause.

"I want to set the pace this time," I tell him. Communication is key… I know we won't get far here unless I tell Oliver exactly what I want.

"I'll do whatever you want, baby. Take whatever you need," he moans as I work myself onto his shaft.

This position feels different and allows him to go deeper. I can tell he is trying so hard not to thrust or move and I appreciate it as I adjust to this new feeling. Once he is completely inside me up to the hilt, I gasp at how full I feel, focusing on it. The first time, there was pain and an awkwardness. Now, all I can feel is Oliver.

He is staring at where our bodies are now connected, a bead of sweat forming on his brow. Fuck. Oh the strength this man has.

"Sorry," I mutter, slowly beginning to rock back and forth.

"Don't you apologize," he moans, his eyes sliding closed for just a moment. "Damn baby you feel so good."

I ride him like that for a while, his hands simply moving with me on my hips. I decide I like how this position feels, but I want Oliver to be in control.

"I want to change positions," I pant into his ear. "I want you to fuck me."

I surprise myself with how crass the sentence is that comes out of my mouth. I gasp and he chuckles, a low, guttural noise. Almost a growl escapes from his lips as he easily flops me onto my back as if I weigh nothing. Never in my wildest dreams did I ever think any man would be able to throw *me* around like a rag doll, but here we are.

Oliver stands and drags me to the edge of the bed, grabbing my legs and pressing each to his chest on either side of his head. For a moment he plays with my clit with his thumb. With his other hand he's grabbing a condom from who knows where, ripping it open and sliding it onto himself. Oops. I completely forgot about that. At least someone is being responsible here.

Once the condom is on he focuses both hands on me, one reaching forward to play with the hardened peak of my nipple. Always the tease. I moan with my head back in the sheats, about ready to beg when he shoves inside of me. He buries himself in one thrust this time and I squeal at the suddenness of it.

He pauses, his eyes roaming over my face. He's afraid he's hurt me.

"I'm okay," I gasp. "Please, Oliver, fuck me."

That's all the go ahead he needed.

"You are so fucking perfect, Stella," he moans as he slides almost completely out and then thrusts back in. I gasp again but this time, he doesn't stop.

His pace is faster and harder than it was the first time. He's not being as gentle with me this time and I love it. I'm not going to last much longer.

"That feels so good," I pant.

"The way you sound drives me mad," he moans, his eyes sliding shut as his pace increases.

That is all that it takes. I am a spring wound up and I am finally letting go. The world goes black and I see stars behind my eyelids. I am pretty sure my screams are probably going to wake up both Nat and Caleb but I don't care.

When I finally begin to come down from the feeling of the most amazing orgasm I could ever imagine, I open my eyes to see Oliver beginning to chase after his own.

Watching Oliver come is something I will never get tired of. The way his muscles tense and his eyes slide almost shut, his mouth partially open. His moans fill the room and then he is tensing, his speed becoming sloppy.

I find myself smiling tiredly as he lays down beside me, wrapping an arm around me and pulling me tightly against him.

He kisses the top of my head, his breathing heavy and matching my own.

Neither of us say anything. Neither of us need to. Eventually, I curl my body closer to his and lay my head on his chest. He's mindlessly stroking his fingers through my hair, only the sound of our own breathing filling our ears.

"Hey, Olly," I say after what feels like hours have passed.

"Yeah?"

"Can I ask you something?"

"Literally anything." He laughs gently. "There isn't a single thing I would hide from you."

I smile, enjoying his answer more than I'd like to admit. Taking a deep breath, I contemplate whether I should take advantage of his honesty to ask some big question. There are still so many things I don't know about him and that he doesn't know about me. Despite the journals, despite the hours we've spent together, I know I will spend forever learning who Olly is inside and out.

So instead of ruining the moment, I tuck my chin against his chest so that I can see his face and I smile, deciding to go with my original question.

"Would you rather have carrots for fingers or potatoes for feet?"

He immediately dissolves into a fit of laughter, shaking my entire body with his vibrations.

"Carrots. That way I can eat my fingers if I get hungry."

"You could eat potato feet." I argue.

"Yeah but who wants to eat raw potatoes?"

We dissolve into a round of laughter riddled would you rathers as my eyes grow heavy.

Chapter Nineteen

I wake up curled up beside Olly. He's still sleeping, his chest rising and falling steadily. I don't want to move. The last thing I want to do is disturb this moment but I have to pee. So I don't have a choice.

Slowly, I unravel myself from his arms. He doesn't wake up, even as I kiss his forehead.

I don't wake him up before I leave.

I know I should, but I don't have any clothes here save for my bathing suit, and I want to get home before the town wakes up too much.

I jog across the street and let myself into my Aunt's, using the hidden key from outfront.

She must still be sleeping, which is good. I don't want to talk about whatever she and Olly discussed yesterday. At least not yet.

After showering and brushing my hair, I pull on jean shorts and a t-shirt. It feels odd, not having my journal here to jot my thoughts in before starting my day. A smile plays on the corner of my lips at the thought of Oliver reading through it. Maybe he's doing just that right now. How odd that the thought doesn't make me nervous anymore. I want Oliver to know all that there is to know about me. Just as I now know him.

I don't have work today and it is supposed to be stormy and gross today.

It's not raining yet, so I grab my earbuds, plug them into my phone, and jog back across the street to the beach. There is hardly anyone here. The sky is dark and the waves are crashing against the beach with a violence that assumes the day is going to be nasty.

I like the wind and darkness.

I sit down in the sand and press play on a murder podcast Nat recommended to me, closing my eyes to listen to the words.

I am so lost in the story about a girl found in some backwoods of Kentucky that I jump when someone taps a finger on my shoulder.

Once I get over the initial shock of it, I shake my shoulders out and breathe deeply. It's probably Oliver.

When I look over my shoulder though, I immediately rip my earbuds out and jump to my feet. It isn't Oliver. It's Leo.

"What are you doing here?" I ask, looking over his shoulder, expecting to see Beth. I know they aren't together anymore, but why else would he be here?

"I'm alone," he mutters, running a hand through his hair. He looks off, his eyes bloodshot and his hands shaking. His normally pulled together attire is replaced with baggy jeans and a stained white top.

He reeks of alcohol. Is he really drunk at nine o'clock in the morning?

"Leo," I try again, keeping my voice level. "What are you doing here?"

"I was an idiot, Stella," he slurs, taking a step closer to me. I counter that step with my own backward. I don't want him any closer to me. He's clearly drunk. Sober, he's kind of an asshole. Drunk, I'm not sure what he's capable of. I glance up towards the road. Of course it's the first stormy day we've had since I've been here and the town is all but dead. The only others on the beach are a group of high schoolers on the other end taking photos of each other in front of the crashing waves.

If I needed to, would they hear me yelling? I doubt it. The waves are loud.

A raindrop hits my cheek and I flinch.

"Leo, you're drunk." I say slowly. "Let me help you get back home. Did you drive here?"

"I was an idiot in High School. I hope you can forgive me for what I did. You were the best thing that ever happened to me." He reaches his hand out to brush my cheek and I take another step back. "Do you remember when you loved for me to touch you?"

"Leo, that was four years ago. We've both moved on. I forgive you," as I say it, I can feel the weight of the words settling in my gut. I do forgive him but not because he deserves it. Simply because it doesn't matter to me anymore. I know I am so much more than what happened between him and I.

"You're going to have a baby with Beth, Leo. I'm in a relationship. Everything else is in the past. Okay?"

"None of that matters! I haven't moved on," his voice is growing louder. "I don't know how I never saw it before. You, Stella, are perfect. Where was this confidence in High School? I never would have let you go."

He reaches out and before I can stop him, grabs me by the elbows and pulls me to him.

"Leo, let me go," I try to pull myself away, but he's holding on tightly, his fingers digging into the skin on my arms. I yank again. Should I scream?

"Calm down, Stella," his whisper reeks of alcohol, wafting over my face as he pulls me close. His face is an inch from mine. I pull back as far as I can. "Don't you miss this? Miss us?"

"No, Leo. Let me go." I speak firmly, but he doesn't waver.

"Stella!" Caleb's voice shouts from across the beach. He's walking quickly from their apartment. "You okay?"

Just as I'm about to answer, three things happen at the exact same time. Leo leans in, his lips crushing against mine, fingers digging roughly into my cheek. Just as they do, a loud crack whips him off his feet, crashing back into the sand. The impact knocks me off my own feet and I fall back too, landing with a thud on my ass.

Caleb is now sprinting in our direction, but my eyes aren't on him anymore.

Oliver is punching Leo into the sand.

He is kneeling over him and his fists are flying, an anger I have never seen painted on his face.

"Oliver!" I shout, struggling to my feet.

"Stop him, Stella!" Caleb is shouting. His feet can't carry him any faster.

In a desperate attempt, I hurl myself at Oliver's back, pulling at him, but he easily shakes me off. In the glimpse I get into his eyes, my stomach drops into my feet. He is beyond reason. The man standing before me isn't a man I have ever met.

"Oliver! Listen to me!" Caleb finally reaches us, throwing himself between Oliver and Leo. Leo is a whimpering, bloody mess in the sand. He is holding his face with one hand and his shoulder with the other.

Oliver tries to push through Caleb, but Caleb stands firm, holding his hands up.

"I don't want to fight you, Olly, but I will."

"He deserves it." Oliver spits. "Did you see what he was doing?"

"I did, and I'm not saying he doesn't!" Caleb shouts back. "But he isn't worth it. Do you really want to go back to jail for this guy?"

"For her? Any day!" He points at me.

I am shivering and sobbing and terrified. A pair of arms wrap around me. I barely comprehend that they belong to Aunt Milly.

She is tugging me across the street. Sirens are wailing. A small crowd has formed. Caleb is pushing

Oliver farther back and he is staring at me over his friend's shoulder. He is saying something but I can't hear him. He's yelling to me. I want to go to him but I don't. I allow Aunt Milly to tug me away, unable to get that anger out of my head. For a moment, Oliver wasn't the man I love.

And that terrifies me.

Chapter Twenty

"Leo isn't going to press any charges," Nat's voice comes over the phone, slow and soft. "His dad is coming to pick him up tonight."

I nod, feeling numb.

Oliver was taken by the cops to the local station and put behind bars for the night. My stomach and head are a mess. I can't get the image of Leo's bloody face out of my head. What's worse - I can't get Oliver's angry face out either. I had no idea he was capable of such violence.

Do I even know the guy I thought I loved?

"Stella," Nat says my name softly. "Oliver wants to see you. He keeps asking-"

"Nat, I can't."

"He was protecting you, Stella. If Caleb had gotten their first he would be the one behind bars right now. Hell, if I had-"

"But you didn't, Nat." I choke up a light sob. "Oliver did. I…I think he would have killed him, Nat. You didn't see his face."

A long stretch of silence follows.

"You don't know what Leo is capable of either, Stella," she finally reasons. "That's what we do when the people we care about are in danger. I'm sorry if you wouldn't do the same."

The phone clicks and I am alone, plunged into the silence. It doesn't last long as Aunt Milly climbs the stairs to the attic and sits on the end of my bed. She pushes a strand of hair behind her ear, taking a deep breath as she contemplates what to say.

I'm not sure what to expect from her. I would have expected Nat to stand up for Oliver. It didn't even come as a surprise when she called.

Is Aunt Milly going to rub it in my face? Am I about to hear "I told you so"? She was the one who warned me to stay away from him in the beginning. Maybe she's regretting taking that back.

"What happened with Leo, honey?" She asks instead.

"He wouldn't stop. He wouldn't take no for an answer. Then he kissed me," I summarize the short interaction, squeezing my eyes shut tight to block it out. The feeling of his hands on my face, holding me against him. I flinch at the thought. "Nat says he isn't pressing charges against Oliver."

"I would sure think not," she lets out an aggravated sigh, throwing her hands in the air. "Who knows what would have happened if Oliver hadn't shown up."

I look up then, making eye contact with her.

I am too tired to think. I am too tired to talk reason with her, to hear her thinking or to even care. It is only eleven in the morning and I feel like I've been up for days. I lay back in bed, closing my eyes and pulling the blankets up over me.

"I need to be alone for a bit." I mutter.

I don't hear Aunt Milly's reply. I'm not sure if she even does, but I feel the bed shift and I know I am alone.

*   *   *

When I finally drag myself out of bed the next morning, throw on jeans and a t-shirt, and slump down the stairs, I'm shocked to see that Aunt Milly isn't alone.

Caleb is sitting at the dining room table, leaned back in his chair with his arms crossed. As if his appearance wasn't enough of a shock, sitting across from him is my mother. She looks just as irritated and entirely out of place. Aunt Milly is leaning against the sink with a cup of tea in her hands, looking oddly amused.

"Good morning, Stell-Bells," Aunt Milly gives me a tired, sorry smile.

"It's too early for this," I groan, dragging myself to the coffee pot and praying no one will try to talk to me before I get at least one sip to my lips.

My prayer does not get answered. Big surprise.

"Honey, aren't you going to say hi to your mother?" My mom referring to herself in the third person is something I wish I could say I wasn't used to.

I pour the coffee and turn around before answering her.

"Of course I'm happy to see you mom, but what are you doing here?"

She doesn't look offended, unfortunately. It doesn't seem right to have her here. She doesn't fit into this home or this town. My body feels itchy and strange knowing she's infiltrated my perfect little escape. Yesterday comes crashing back and I'm hit suddenly by the realization that my escape isn't so perfect anymore. It was already shattered before she showed up.

I feel sick.

"Once Leo's family was contacted, news traveled fast. That boy you brought home with you beat him up? I knew he was trouble."

Caleb pounds his fist on the table and startles both of us. Mom jumps and my head whips around to face him. Aunt Milly is completely still. Calm.

"Caleb," I warn.

His jaw clenches, but he keeps his mouth shut.

"Anyway," mom looks back at me, rolling her shoulders. "Your father and I thought it would be easier for you to come home if I was here to help."

It was my turn to act shocked.

I sat my mug down and crossed my arms.

"Who said I was going home?" I glance over at Aunt Milly, but she shakes her head. That amused smile is still on her lips. Oh. So she knew why mom was here. She knew this was about to be a shit show.

Thanks for the warning Aunt Milly.

"Well no one. But obviously you don't want anything to do with this place anymore, right? You want to come home to thought and reason."

I tilt my head to the side, searching my own mind for the answer. Do I want to go home? The answer should be yes, right? I know for a fact that there was a time it would have been. Running has always seemed easier than facing my problems head on, hence why I am even here.

"No mom," I finally answer. "I'm not going anywhere. I am home."

The only way I can describe her reaction is that of a chicken ruffling up its feathers. She stands and her back straightens, her arms falling flat against her sides.

"Honey, Oliver isn't good for you. This place isn't good for you. Just look at what it's done to you." She waves a hand at all of me.

What is that supposed to mean?

"Mom," I step forward and close the distance between myself and Caleb. "I love you. So much. And I want to talk to you. But not right now and not about this. You'll excuse us."

I grab Caleb's hand and pull him to his feet. He follows me out the front door and the screen creaks behind us on the way out.

*   *   *

"Where is he?" I ask Caleb the moment we leave the front porch.

"Stella, I know you are mad at him. I know he scared you, I know you don't think you know him. I know…. But Stella, he needs you and-"

"Caleb," I snap. He looks up at me mid rant, his lips sealing into a tight line. "Where is he?"

"I came over to convince you to come see him. Nat said you didn't want to see him. You want to know where he is?"

"I didn't want to see him yesterday. I needed time to think. I'm not even sure this is a good idea right now but I've never been all that great at good ideas anyway," I run a hand through my hair. "So yeah. Where is he?"

"His room," Caleb tells me. He's assessing me, looking for some kind of answer.

I'm not sure it's one he's ever going to find since I'm not sure I even have my own answers.

"Thank you," I tell him as we walk across the road towards their apartment.

"You don't have to thank me for telling you where Olly is, Stella. You know you're always welcome."

"Not for that," I shake my head. "I know yesterday could have been so much worse if you hadn't been there."

Caleb bites down on his lower lip as we near the front door. Pausing before opening it, he places a hand on my shoulder and lowers his voice.

"There's some things I don't think you quite know about Olly's past, Stella. We all have things. Just remember that, okay? Even the people we love. They aren't perfect."

I'm just about to disappear inside on my search for Oliver, the only thing I care about right now, when my phone vibrates in my pocket.

I don't want to answer it. I almost don't even pull it from my pocket. But I have been trying so hard all summer to stop being so selfish. So instead, I pause beside the door and grab my phone from my back pocket.

Caleb pauses with me, crossing his arms over his chest and raising an eyebrow.

Malory's name and smiling face beam up at me from my phone. Again, I almost don't answer. We haven't talked since the baby shower; whatever she has to say can probably wait. On the other hand, we haven't talked since the baby shower. What if something is wrong?

"I'll go inside in a minute," I tell Caleb who is still waiting for me to make a move. "I promise I won't run off. Thank you again, Caleb. You're a good friend."

He reaches out and squeezes my arm before disappearing inside the house. Once he's inside, I press answer and hold the phone to my ear.

"Hey Stella," Malory's voice is calm but there is an edge to it. An undertone that normally isn't there. I straighten my back, preparing for the worse.

"Hey. Is everything okay?"

"I wanted to warn you," She says, the words coming out in a bit of a rush. "But I didn't think sending a text would be very kind."

"Warn me about what?" My eyebrows crinkle together. As if today hasn't already been crazy enough and it only just started.

"Your mom is on her way."

"Oh, I know," I sigh. If that's all she was calling to warn me about, we're in the clear. I already knew that. "She ambushed me when I got out of bed this morning."

"That's not all," she groans. "Daven is with her. And Leo's dad. They all rode up together."

Leo's dad doesn't surprise me. I knew he was coming and word spreads fast in our small town. It's not surprising he and my mom chose to carpool up together. But Daven?

"What's Daven doing here?" I glance around the beach as if he might jump out at me. I don't see his car at the curb by Aunt Milly's or parked in the free parking outside the beach.

"He didn't want you to be alone when your mom got there. I promise he's not on her side, Stella." Mallory breaths out, as if satisfied that she's finally told me what she called to say.

"Why are you warning me?"

"Your mom has never seen me in the best light, Stella, but she's not a bad person. She doesn't agree with every decision you make and it's hard for her to see someone she loves so much making decisions she wouldn't make."

"So…you're defending her?"

Never would I have ever thought Malory would be on my mom's side. The two of them, while civil most of the time, also had moments when putting them in the same room was an incredibly bad idea. It took mom months to see Malory as a member of the family, even after her and Daven were engaged. Part of me always wondered if it was because they got engaged so young. Her and dad had been young too. Maybe she regretted it.

But what I was doing here had nothing to do with any of that.

"No," Malory states firmly. "I am on your side too, Stella, if there are sides. I'm only saying that she's still your mom and she still loves you. She's just struggling to believe someone could be happy making choices she wouldn't make. In her own weird way, she's trying to protect you."

I take a deep breath.

I can see what she is saying. My mom and I have butted heads since I dropped from College more than we haven't. She pushed me here just to get rid of me while simultaneously believing this place could be bad for me. However, it wasn't always like this. My mother and I used to be so close, she was the person

I went to for almost everything. I can't remember those days well anymore, but I know they existed and I refuse to believe I'll never get them back.

Maybe Malory is right.

"Thank you," I say, meaning it.

"Of course. I love you, Stella."

"I love you too."

Once the call disconnects, I stuff my phone back in my pocket and look out at the ocean for what feels like a very long time.

My mind is a mess. My thoughts are being pulled in a million different directions but I am only sure of one train of thought and that is the one that leads to Oliver.

I take a deep, calming breath, letting the salt air rush into my lungs. Once I feel a tad more steady I turn for the door.

Chapter Twenty-One

The last time I closed Oliver's bedroom door behind me and locked it, we had sex. That fact is burning a hole in my mind as I twist the lock and swallow, hard. I'm still not entirely sure what I am doing here.

Oliver is sitting on his bed with his head leaned up against his headboard. He doesn't stand when I enter the room. In fact, he barely moves his head. His knuckles are bruised and he looks exhausted.

Does it make me insane that I want to hold him? All I want to do suddenly is comfort him.

"What happened all of those years ago, Olly?" I finally whisper, clasping and unclasping my hands together in front of me. I am nervous in a way I haven't been around Oliver since we first met. My heart is pounding inside my chest and my hands are growing clammy.

I force the panic away, knowing that's not how it works but willing any anxiety to leave me alone. My heart rate continues to increase and my vision is growing blurry.

"Stella," he whispers, his voice low. "I won't apologize for what I did yesterday. He deserved it."

I shake my head.

"Please. Answer the question."

The room is spinning and the ground is getting closer. I stumble a step and then another before taking a seat on the edge of the bed. The moment I do, Oliver stands and walks around so that he is facing me.

"I thought your Aunt would have told you last night."

I shake my head, unable to speak. Any words are caught in my throat or on my dry tongue. If he doesn't start giving me answers soon, I might pass out. I wonder if he can tell I am mid panic attack.

Just as I wonder it, he drops to his knees in front of me and grabs my hands.

"Stella, please don't be scared of me." He begs.

Even in my panicked state, my eyebrows shoot up. My nerves sooth for a second if only out of confusion.

"I'm not." I tell him.

"You're not?"

"Olly, I could never be scared of you. Leo is an asshole. Did he deserve to have his face beat in? I'm not sure. But am I mad that you did it?" Am I? I hadn't let myself be alone with my thoughts for long, drowning them out with either music or sleep.

As I focus on the feeling of Oliver's hands holding mine, listen to the waves outside his open window, look into his honest and trusting eyes, my own heartbeat begins to settle and I know the answer.

"I was terrified you were going to get yourself in trouble, Oliver. And part of that is because you still have secrets from your past you haven't told me." I pull one of my hands away to rake it through my hair. "Apparently my Aunt deserved to know, but not me?"

"Milly already knew what happened. I wanted to give her my side of the story before I told you."

"Why?" I whispered.

Oliver pauses for a moment before answering. His hands slide from mine to rest on my knees instead and he takes a deep breath, clenching his jaw as he thinks.

"I'm afraid once you know how fucked up my past is…how fucked up I can be, you're going to run."

His words shock me so much, I feel my eyebrows pop right up into my hairline. Isn't that the same thing I've been fearing all along? That I wasn't good enough. That my past was too complicated. Aren't those the things Oliver has been actively trying to convince me are not true? How can't he see that in himself?

Another fear takes root in my stomach.

How bad can his secret be? And worse, why can I not think of a single scenario in which something he had done would make me stop loving him?

"Oliver, tell me." I whisper.

His head drops to my knees for a moment, resting there. I fight the urge to run my fingers through his hair, to tell him he has nothing to worry about, I'm not going anywhere.

"The year after Chris killed himself was a dark one for me," He starts, pulling his head up and moving to sit beside me instead of on the floor. I shift to get a better look at his face, even as his head is dipped down.

"You've told me. Vandalism and drugs, right?"

"Right." He nods, but there's more. "I was also dealing with a lot of anger. After we graduated High School, I was lost. I had no idea how to control it and I didn't want to listen to anyone who was trying to help me find a way. I blamed myself for his death and it didn't matter what anyone said. It was my fault. Tom was able to pull Caleb back from the edge and I was no longer doing any drugs, but I still had so much anger. So I started fighting in some underground rings."

"Here?" My question comes out as a squeak.

He nods, his eyes tired and weary.

"Caleb came with me but he never fought. He was always there to back me down when I got a bit too out of hand. I wasn't good at knowing when to stop. I was out of control."

"This was before Tom stepped in?"

He nods again.

"Tom bailed me out of jail more times than I like to admit. I didn't have a family who cared and most adults around here were sick of me. I was spiraling. I'd punch a guy on the sidewalk just for looking at me wrong."

I swallow hard.

I find it hard to believe that he's talking about the same guy sitting before me now.

"Nat started seeing this guy, James Humphrey. He was from out of town, here for college, and she fell hard. This was before she met Carrie. She was spending all of her time with him for months. One night we were all at a bonfire party on the beach and she pulled Caleb and I to the side. She said she was scared of him, that he'd started putting his hands on her and she didn't know how far he was going to go. She made us promise we wouldn't do anything and that she was going to break up with him the next day. I wasn't going to, I swear. But I drank too much and by the time the party was winding to an end, I spotted him walking off alone towards his car."

Silence surrounds us. I wait with baited breath, unwilling to even move a muscle. I feel as if I know everything about Oliver and nothing at all in this moment.

"He looked so sure of himself, so cocky. It pissed me off, knowing what he had done to Nat. I'll spare you the details, but I got lucky. He was in the hospital for over a week. Tom didn't even want to bail me out this time at first, until Caleb told him what James had done. He chose not to press charges and Tom was able to grease some palms. I paid desperately for that night."

I swallowed, unwilling to speak until I knew for certain he was done.

"Nobody looked at me the same for a long time. James was an innocent college kid and I was the street fighter who couldn't control himself. That's the story your aunt knew and that's the story most people around here love to tell. I should have told you sooner. Before it came to this."

Gnawing on my bottom lip, I search my brain for what to say. What is there to say? I'm not afraid of you. I don't think you did anything wrong. We all make mistakes but yours seems pretty justified. Am I insane for thinking all of those things?

Before I'm able to answer though, there's a knock on his bedroom door. Neither of us move to answer it, our eyes locked, our knees just barely touching. Somehow, this moment feels more intimate than any we've had before. I am acutely aware of my body and my breathing.

"Stella. It's Beth. She's here." Surprisingly, it's Nat's voice that comes from the other side of the door.

Unwillingly, I pull my attention from Oliver and stand up. What is Beth doing here?

He grabs my hand and I pause, looking down at him. I search his eyes, but I can't read them. Someone who has been so honest and open since the moment I met him suddenly feels like a closed case that I don't have the rights to read. I feel tears pricking at the backs of my eyes, but I blink them away, refusing to cry.

"I'll be back, okay?"

Just before I turn to go, I lean down and peck a kiss on his lips. It's quick and our lips barely touch. And then I dart out the door.

*   *   *

"Are you okay?" Nat asks as we jog down the stairs into the living room. I am smoothing out the non existent wrinkles on my shirt. I can't keep my hands still. It feels as if an entire week has happened in just a couple of days. I need a moment to think.

It becomes obvious that I'm not going to get one when I walk out onto the beach to find not only Beth waiting for me, but also my mother, Leo's father, and Daven. Beth and Daven are standing beside each other and Leo's father and my mother are standing together. Like two united fronts, both against me.

I can feel Nat standing behind me as the front door closes, and I take from her strength.

"Daven, Beth," my brow furrows as I try not to jump to conclusions. I'm also not going to give away to Daven that his wife warned me he was coming. Whether he knows or not, I'll keep it our little secret. "What are you guys doing here?"

"We heard what happened and I had to come," Beth is biting down on her lower lip, looking around as if this is the last place she wants to be. "Make sure you are alright."

"And that Leo was." Nat snapped from behind me.

"Nat-" I start to defend Beth. There is no way she really came to check on Leo. But her face tells me the opposite the moment I open my mouth. "Is that true, Beth? Did you come to check on me, or Leo?"

"Can't it be both?" She mutters, looking down at her feet instead of up at me.

I barely hear the door open behind us. Caleb and Oliver walk out together. At the sight of Oliver, my mother's back straightens and a frown forms. Beth continues to look weary. Leo's dad and Daven both look as if they don't want to be here.

"Who's side are you on, Daven?" I ask my brother, feeling an unexpected anger at him rise in my chest. My brother has always been my safe haven. When I'm not sure what to do, I go to him. When I have nowhere else to go, I go to his home. So the thought that he might be here with mom to drag me back to a home I no longer belong in makes my stomach churn with anger. I know Malory said that wasn't the case, but how am I to be sure?

"I don't see sides here, sis," He speaks loudly and clearly and only to me. "But if I did, you know I'd always be on yours."

"Honey, let's go talk somewhere in private," my mom steps forward, grabbing my arm, but I yank it back.

"Anything you have to say you can say here," I tell her. I feel stronger here with Nat, Oliver and Caleb at my back. I feel a hand on the small of my back and I lean into it. Oliver is warm and strong and mine. His past doesn't matter to me just as much as mine didn't matter to him.

I only wish I'd been able to tell him that.

I wish he hadn't been afraid to tell me about it before now.

"Fine," mom's back straightens, her hands folding at her waist, and I know I'm about to receive a heavy blow. I prepare myself, forming my lips into a thin line and sucking in a deep breath through my nose. "You clearly are not safe here, Stella. I am your mother and I am only looking out for your safety. I warned you about this place and the things that it will do to you, but hanging out with people like this?" She waves her finger up at Oliver, including Nat and Caleb in on the accusation. "Well honey it's not just concerning anymore. You need to come home."

"Please listen to your mother, Stella," Beth whispers. It's as if she doesn't want anyone else to hear. But they all can. And we are all looking at her now. "I don't want what happened to me to happen to you."

"It won't, Beth," I whisper back. For some reason, this feels private.

While my mother is attacking me and blowing the entire thing out of proportion, maybe Beth in some odd way really does care. She's been through so much… who am I to even pretend to understand where she is coming from? I wish we were alone so I could pull her to me and tell her the past doesn't matter. What matters is how we all choose to move forward. But that also feels private, so I keep my mouth shut and simply look into her eyes instead.

Hers are brimming with tears just as I am sure mine are.

"Your situation was different than Stella's, Beth," it's my Aunt Milly's voice that joins the conversation now, coming from up the beach. She smiles gently at me before turning to the others. "Putting that on her isn't fair, sweetie. Oliver is a good kid." She turns to my mom now. "Elanor, do you really think, as your sister and her Aunt, that I would let her hang around him if he wasn't?"

Silence falls over the entire group.

We aren't meeting a happy place. Not now and probably not anytime soon.

I finally know what I want and I am not going to stand for people telling me I can't have it. I want Oliver. I want to live here.

"I love you guys," I step forward and pull my mom into an awkward hug. At first her body is stiff and unwelcoming, but eventually, her arms wrap around me and she squeezes back. "I love you mom," I whisper in her ear. "But I am staying here. I love this place, and I love him."

When I pull back, I don't look at her face. I don't want to see what emotion is written there. I don't want to fight anymore.

"Come here," I pull Beth in for a hug, squeezing tight. I'm not sure what to say to her. If she's here to check in on Leo that definitely complicates our friendship further. But I don't want to deal with it right now and suddenly, it doesn't matter that much to me. "Call me."

Pulling back, I refuse to look her in the eye. I can not start crying. If anyone here has the power to completely derail me, it's Beth.

Time between us, pasts behind us, terrible decisions still at our feet, one thing will always be true - Beth is my best friend. I'm not sure how we are going to fix what is so broken here, but we will. I now know without a shadow of a doubt that nothing is too broken to be fixed.

I give her a final squeeze and turn to my brother. He's hard to read, as usual, but he looks pleased. I hope he isn't mad with the choices I'm making. As sure of them as I am, my people pleasing self might not be able to handle disappointing him.

Giving Daven a hug, I hold onto him the longest.

"I'm proud of you, sis," he whispers into my hair. I feel my entire body relax.

I leave the beach with my hand wrapped in Oliver's. I'm not sure where we're going or what we are going to do, and I don't care.

"Your past doesn't matter to me," I say, looking up at Oliver as we cross the road, heading directly for my car parked on the curb. "There is nothing you could ever do that would make me love you any less, Oliver."

His smile is breathtaking. Every bit of tension that has followed us around since Leo showed up evaporates. I can almost see it rolling off of our shoulders and out into the ocean, being swept away with the tide.

"I love you Stella."

I squeeze his hand and we continue to my car in silence. Are we being watched as we walk away? I can almost imagine Caleb pumping his fist into the air and Nat giving the group a smug smirk. I hold back my own smirk as I realize I just claimed this place as home. I hope Aunt Milly is watching us walk away with pride. I made a decision entirely for myself.

And I intend to continue making them.

I am starting a new list.

10 things to do before I go - 1. Kiss Oliver until I can't breathe.

And that is exactly what we go off to do.

Chapter Twenty-Two

"You don't have to say anything, Stella. I'm telling you. Oliver knows." Caleb shakes his head from the passenger seat of my car. He's smiling, but it's a humorless smile that doesn't quite meet his eyes. We're carpooling home from our shift and it's getting dark out. The bonfire party Nat decided to host for the end of the summer should be in full swing when we get to the beach house. Oliver will be waiting there too. My stomach is assaulted with butterflies at the thought of seeing him again, even though I saw him just this morning. Am I ever going to get used to calling him mine?

"Are you sure he doesn't think I hate him?" I slap the steering wheel, resisting the urge to scream. "Should I tell him again that I think he did the right thing with Leo? Should I thank him again?"

Caleb raises an eyebrow and shakes his head. I just spent our entire shift explaining to him how for the past week since my mom showed up I have done nothing but thank Oliver. Thank you, I'm sorry, I love you. Somehow, it still doesn't feel like enough. I think I'll spend my entire life explaining to Oliver how much he means to me and it'll never feel like enough. Oddly though, I'm okay with that.

"I think you're good." He laughs, again, a sound that holds no humor. "I also think you should go to Nat with this girly shit from now on. I'll gossip with you whenever Stella, but talking about my best friend's love life is where I draw the line."

He's joking, even though his tone is flat.

Something isn't quite right. He's twisting that tattered old black ball cap in his hands, squeezing it so tightly I'm afraid he's going to ruin it for good.

"Is everything okay?" I finally ask, pushing my own feelings to the back burner. I've spent so long talking about myself, I didn't even quite realize just how dark the circles are under Caleb's eyes. He hasn't had his same peppy step or flirty attitude today either. Now that I think of it, he kind of just slid through the day without making a single jab at me, no matter how many opportunities I gave him.

Caleb shrugs, looking out the window for a second. His grip tightens on that stupid hat, bending the bill even farther in on itself.

"If you're not careful you're going to break that. Maybe then I can finally buy you a new one," I laugh, hoping to cut some of the new tension in the air. Caleb is always so upbeat and happy; I hate to see him like this.

"Today's my birthday. Our birthday." He glances down at the hat again and then throws me one of his famous smiles. "Don't get me a new hat, please. It belonged to Chris."

My heart sinks into my toes.

No matter how much Oliver has told me about Chris, I have never heard Caleb talk about him. Of course I know they were twins, of course I know his death must have impacted Caleb maybe even harder than it did Oliver, but I guess I just never gave it much thought.

Tears prickle at the back of my eyes.

"I am so sorry, Caleb. I can't imagine-"

"Don't, please," Caleb holds a hand up, using the other to twist the hat back onto his head. "I am sick of people feeling sorry for me. I just want my brother back."

I slam my mouth shut and gulp over a large lump in my throat.

"Sorry, that was harsh. I just mean we don't make a big deal about my birthday anymore. It's not a day I especially enjoy."

I nod, gripping the steering wheel tightly. I have no idea what to say. Caleb and I are good friends, but I've never seen him like this. Nat or Oliver would be better suited for this situation. I don't want to say sorry again and I don't want to say happy birthday, so instead I just begin to sing along to the song playing quietly on the radio.

Caleb looks back out his window and the tension that had joined us for just a moment fades.

I think I'll spend forever learning the secrets of this town.

*   *   *

Dusk is setting in over the ocean, casting a gray glow as I pull my car up to the curb. A bonfire is already roaring in the center of the beach, bodies filing in from the road and from nearby houses. Most of the tourists have left for the season, leaving the locals happy and at ease.

Caleb gets out of the car the second I park and heads straight for a group of people by the fire. I see his dad, Tom, standing among them. The burly man puts a hand on his son's back as soon as he approaches him and his hand doesn't move. Caleb simply stands there as Tom talks to the group he's standing with, staring into the fire with his father's hand grounding him.

I sit for a moment, watching the people I've grown to love over just one summer. Nat is sitting in a camp chair a few feet from the fire, her elbows resting on her knees. She's not talking to anyone and judging by the pinched look on her face, a million thoughts are running through her head.

Aunt Milly is walking across the beach, holding a blanket folded up against her chest, her long blue sundress brushing the sand as she walks.

I'm about to look away from her to find Oliver when I notice something odd. She's spotted someone in the crowd and she's staring at them, a longing look in her eye. My brow furrowing, I follow her gaze, finding Tom staring directly back at her.

The exchange lasts for a split second and I'm sure I'm the only one who noticed. Aunt Milly shakes her shoulders out and turns away, walking towards the lapping tides. Tom stares after her, looking as if he's just seen a ghost. They've both lived here together for years, there is no way they don't know each other. But that look wasn't one acquaintances would share. I'm beginning to rap my brain for what their brief look could mean when I spot Oliver jogging towards me.

His hair is pulled up into a half bun, his skin looking tanner than usual under a black t-shirt. Over one arm is a bright orange blanket. A smile so wide it has the power to make my heart skip a beat is spread over his lips.

I'll ask Aunt Milly about Tom later. Suddenly, at this moment, it doesn't matter.

"Hey, baby," Oliver offers me his hand and I stand from my car, following him down onto the sand. "How was work?"

"Long," I laugh. "I'm ready for this party."

Oliver casts me a humor filled glance and I chuckle, realizing at the same time the irony in my words. I had a panic attack at the first party I ever attended here. The fact that I'm now excited for one has a kind of odd melancholy feeling attached to it.

I've grown so much since first stepping foot in this town. I'm not sure I would even recognize that girl anymore. Realizing this fills me with a strange sadness but it also makes me feel proud. The girl I was before would never have had the strength to stand up for herself the way I did only two weeks ago. She wouldn't have chosen to stay here, even being the only thing she really wanted.

"I'm going to have to start a new list," I wonder out loud. I already mentally did, starting with kissing Oliver until my lungs gave out, but that wasn't something he needed to know. "10 Things to do before I go, living in Maine edition."

Oliver laughs, wrapping an arm around me as we approach the bonfire.

"My list is already started. I don't think I can keep the list of things I want to do with you to just 10 though."

I giggle, sinking down into the sand with him by the warmth of the fire and snuggling up against his chest. He wraps his arms fully around me as laughter and quiet conversation blend into a soft white noise around us.

Caleb sinks down beside Oliver and Nat crawls up beside me. Her head rests gently on my shoulder and I smile over at her. She isn't looking at me but at the ocean.

I follow her gaze.

These people, this place, and this summer make me feel so incredibly at home. I suck in a deep breath and close my eyes. I don't ever want it to end.

Chapter Twenty-Three

The tattoo gun buzzes loudly as I grip Oliver's hand. He isn't even wincing. Tom has ear plugs in, his head banging in rhythm to music we can't hear.

I glance down at the heart being formed on his hip bone and smile.

It was his idea. A matching tattoo to my own.

I glance at Tom again, wondering if he can hear us.

"Tom!" Oliver shouts, as if reading my mind. He doesn't even look up, only adjusting slightly in his chair to get a better angle on his work.

I smile and look up at Oliver.

His hair is down today, falling in waves over his chest. He's shirtless to allow easy access to the spot Tom's tattooing. I resist the urge to drag a hand up his abs and kiss a line to follow.

I can do this whenever I want now, I remind myself.

Oliver is officially mine.

The rest of my stuff is coming over in a U-haul driven by Daven this weekend. I started a full time job at the diner two days ago. I am a Bar Harbor resident now. I've spent the last two weeks since my mom left at Oliver's apartment when I wasn't at work. I'm still living with Aunt Milly, but I have a feeling this is going to happen often.

I just can't stay away from him and he doesn't seem to mind. So I think I'll keep hanging around.

"You know I love you, right?" I say, letting myself fully feel the words. They sink into my bones and circle around my heart.

I love Oliver.

Despite every flaw I think makes me unworthy. Despite every flaw the universe tried to shove in my face that would make him undeserving. Despite everything, I love Oliver, and he is mine.

"I love you, Stella. More than life itself," he wraps a hand around the back of my neck and pulls me against his chest. I close my eyes, listening to the sound of his heartbeat under my ear.

This is living.

Epilogue

Fall is in full swing, turning Maine's treelines into colorful views of orange and red. The air is getting chillier and the beach is often empty now.

A few days ago Aunt Milly sat down beside me on the front porch, wrapped in an olive green shawl. She leaned back and smiled over at me. Oliver was sitting beside me, an arm curling me to his side as he read from a book and I watched the tide coming in.

"How would you two like to help me go through some of the boxes in the basement?" She asked, her tone almost like a song.

We agreed. Now, two days later, we've gathered a little crew. Oliver and Caleb are playing with a discarded pool table in the back corner of the basement while Nat and I help Aunt Milly bring certain boxes up to her bedroom.

She was very specific when we began to help.

"These boxes hold lots of memories I'm not ready to go through yet. Just sit them by my bed and come back down here, please."

Nat lifts a particularly heavy box and I follow her up the stairs with a lighter one. We've made it down the hallway and to her door when the box Nat is carrying slips and she drops it with a thud to the floor. The top pops open and a single letter that looks like it was crammed under the folded edges falls to the floor.

We both know we shouldn't read it. But before I've really thought that through, Nat has picked it up, unfolded the crinkled paper, and we are both scanning the elegant font. It's written in cursive, the pencil slightly faded and smudged.

June 15, 1995
Dear Milly,

Summer is boring without you here. I took our favorite hike alone yesterday and the view just wasn't the same. I miss the click of your camera and the sound of your laugh.

I can't wait until your dad lets you come out here and visit. Maybe this summer I'll be able to save enough for that truck and I'll make the trip down to see you.

Keep my heart safe. Don't forget to write.

Love, Thomas

Nat's mouth pops open as the letter sits between us in her open palm.

"There's no way. Thomas?" She gasps. "Like Tom, Thomas?"

"Thomas is a common name. I'm sure it's someone else," I assure her, grabbing the letter and it back in the box, folding the edges back down over it more carefully this time. I make sure it's tight so no more letters will fall out. And maybe Aunt Milly will never question if we were rifling through her past.

 Nat shrugs and moves on, her moment of intrigue gone in seconds.

 However, I keep thinking about that look I saw Aunt Milly and Tom exchange at the bonfire. It was nothing, or so I had convinced myself. It was, right?

AUNT MILLY'S STORY COMING 2024

ACKNOWLEDGMENTS

First, I want to thank my two very best friends, Cheyenne and Alyssa. Alyssa, you and I have grown together our entire lives and I would not have the confidence I do now if it weren't for our friendship. You have always been my rock in an unstable world and for that I will always be grateful. Cheyenne, I honestly don't remember the moment we became friends. You just showed up one day and have been making my life better every single day since. I could never thank you enough for what you have brought to my life. I want to thank both of you for your patience during this writing process, rereading scene after scene and never expressing how irritating my grammar mistakes were.

Second, I want to thank my parents. Without your unwavering support and belief in me I would never have pursued my dreams. As early as middle school you encouraged me by buying me countless notebooks and pens. In High School this encouragement looked like agreeing with my choice to take extra writing classes and signing me up for writing conferences. You both are the reason I never gave up no matter how many unfinished stories I had sitting in my writing software.

Next, I'd like to thank my sisters. Having sisters is like having built in friends for life. No matter what you do, they are stuck with you. Gabrielle, I can't thank you enough for the countless hours we have sat brainstorming timelines and backstories. Your excitement for my characters sometimes even outranks my own and fuels me to keep writing. I always know I have at least one fan waiting for the next book and that is all I need. Rochelle, although you are admittedly not a big reader, I want to thank you for listening to me ramble on countless car rides into work about characters you've never even heard of. Sometimes all you need to flesh out an idea is a listening ear and you gave me that.

I would also like to thank my nieces. By the time you are old enough to read this book, who knows where this life will have taken me. Maybe I'll have published more books. Maybe this will be my one and only. Either way, you both have given me reasons to keep going more than I can count without even knowing it, and for that, Auntie will always be grateful. You are my rays of sunshine in a sometimes dark world and you always will be.

And last, but most definitely not least, I want to thank my husband, Blaine. We have been through so much since we started dating in 2015. Good, bad, ugly and crazy; I wouldn't change any of it and I wouldn't want to go through this crazy life with anybody else. You show me in a million little ways how much you love me every day, inspiring the tiny acts of kindness I write about in my books. The little things always add up to something so much bigger.